Jill

The Deceivers

To Enid,

With all good wishes,

Jill Maughan.

—

An Armada Original

"Without lies humanity would perish of despair and boredom."

Anatole France – 'The Bloom of Life'

To everyone on the home team but especially my aunt, A. M. Maughan

First published in the U.K. in 1990 in Armada

Armada is an imprint of the Children's Division, part of the Collins Publishing Group, 8 Grafton Street, London W1X 3LA

Copyright © 1990 Jill Maughan

Phototypeset by Input Typesetting Ltd, London Printed and bound in Great Britain by William Collins Sons & Co. Ltd, Glasgow

Conditions of Sale
This books is sold subject to the condition that it shall not, by way of trade or otherwise be lent, re-sold, hired out or otherwise circulated without the publisher's prior consent in any form of binding or cover other than that in which it is published and without a similar condition including this condition being imposed on the subsequent purchaser.

Contents

By Fair Means or Foul   5
The Ideal Pony   13
The Challenge Cup   22
Where Respect is Due   29
The Race   37
Secrets   45
Into the Camp of the Enemy   53
Kay's News   61
Home Truths   70
The Witch's Brew   79
The Great Escape   86
When Sparks Fly   95
To the Rescue   102
Just for the Fun of It   112
Misunderstood?   122

Chapter One
By Fair Means or Foul

"I hate you," said my best friend, Jo Day, as we ambled through the driving rain. I glared at Jo through the trickles of water dripping from her once slick baseball hat. It was the first day of the summer holidays and not an auspicious start.

"It'll change nothing, Jo," I said with feeling, and I meant it then.

"You'll change," shrugged Jo confidently. "You're going to get your own pony this summer and then you're off to some posh old boarding school. I'm telling you, Luce, by this time next year you'll be too lah-di-dah for the likes of me."

"Don't be daft," I said. "Anyway, I don't want to go anywhere and I don't want anything to change. I'd much rather be you than me."

"ME?," repeated Jo. "Oh, c'mon. I'll be stuck here with crazy Janey Squires and 'the gang' while you're playing jolly old lacrosse or whatever it is swanky kids like you do."

"Exactly," I said, shoving her. "You'll be exercising my pony while I'm being ambushed by rich kids with lacrosse sticks."

"I'll write," teased Jo. "I'll get the others to write too and if it is too bad we'll spring you somehow."

"It's not a jail," I groaned though at that time the

prospect of boarding school equalled that of a prison in my mind. We had stopped by the side of the deserted country lane, more concerned with our conversation than with the rain that was soaking us to the skin. I wanted Jo to understand that in my mind at least it was she who was the lucky one, but the sky interrupted us by rumbling ominously.

"Run for it," cried Jo.

We were fortunately only yards from our destination – Long Meadows Riding School, owned by the very eccentric and usually bad tempered Janey Squires. We chased through the gate and had just got across the yard when the thunder fired its first round of ammunition. We dived breathlessly into the porch only to find the inner stable doors were locked. Jo rattled them hard.

"Where's Janey? She's always here at this time!" she muttered as a piercing flash of lightning flashed across the black sky.

"She's bound to be here somewhere," I said. "If you try the tackroom, I'll have a look for her in the barn."

Jo dashed off and I made my way to the hay barn. I had never liked that old hay barn. On a day like this the wind stole through the gaps in the ancient roof and the whole damp interior would ring with a ghostly sound. I cautiously went inside, noticing how the hay bales were scattered with customary untidiness and a pitchfork lay tossed on the floor. There was no sign of Janey.

It crossed my mind that she'd most probably slept in. I turned to go when a rustling in the straw froze me. But it was instantly followed by the reassuring meow sound of Janey's cat, Tig. I sighed with relief.

"Tig," I called to the small tortoiseshell cat who had sidled from the shadows. Tig fixed me with her emerald green eyes and rubbed herself against something protruding palely from the straw. I stepped nearer. My mind groped to identify what it was she was scratching herself against. I silently ticked off the various possibilities, a stone, a riding glove, a lost dandy brush. . . . But then with breath-snatching suddenness I knew it was none of these things. It was a human hand and the ring on the index finger was unmistakably Janey's!

I leapt violently backwards with a yell of fright which sent Tig bounding for cover. I stumbled blindly after her, blundering into bales and tripping over the pitch fork. Outside, I ran for all my worth. I burst through the tackroom door. "Janey's dead!" I cried.

Jo was kneeling by the fireplace with sticks in her hand and she gazed blankly at me for what felt like forever. "C'mon. Quick," I urged. "Come and see for yourself!" We ran back to the barn but once inside we skidded to a hesitant stop. I pointed to the pale hand and wrist sticking out from behind the wall of bales and Jo said, "We'd better look. She might just be asleep."

"In the hay barn?" I asked sarcastically. "In the middle of a storm . . . are you mad?"

"Well," shrugged Jo defensively. "She is a bit strange, isn't she?"

"I suppose . . . ," I said thoughtfully. We moved slowly towards the walls of bales and stared apprehensively down at the prostrate form of Janey Squires. She did look dead. Her make up was stark and too doll-like against her ashen skin. Her thin lips were outlined in 'shocking pink' lipstick and formed striking contours for a mouth that hung loosely open.

"She looks dreadful," gasped Jo and, as we moved nearer, Jo pushed her toe into Janey's ribs.

"Don't," I hissed. "She might be very ill, you shouldn't kick ill people."

"I didn't kick her," replied Jo. "I nudged her – like this."

"Urrghr," groaned Janey Squires as Jo's foot contacted with her ribs for the second time. I gave Jo a filthy look but it was entirely lost on her.

"See," she said proudly. "It's done the trick."

Janey was coughing and trying to spit out a piece of straw that had managed to force a path part way down her throat. Her eyes had pricked open and we watched with earnest interest, as the lids fluttered like moths' wings against the light before settling into two little slits in her head.

"Can we get you anything?" I asked.

Janey stared blankly at me before replying then she croaked, "A cigarette." Jo shot me a telling glance as she took the keys to the stables and went to fetch Janey's cigarettes. It wasn't the request either of us had expected from some one close to death's door. The current fashion for health and fitness which outlawed smoking, had completely by-passed Janey Squires. She clung to her old bad habits with the same gritty compulsion that made her cling to her failing riding school business. By the time Jo had returned I'd got Janey into a sitting position. She lit her cigarette with trembling hands and drew purposefully on it. It was a few minutes before she spoke. "I had one of my dizzy spells," she explained as she smoked. "And it's little wonder that I did, what with all the work I've to do around this place, but you two are good girls, aren't you? I know I can rely on you both to help me, especially this summer."

"Why this summer?" Jo asked bluntly.

"Because this summer we have a battle on our hands," retorted Janey. She was rapidly regaining something of her old volatile self.

"Angelica Kent and that riding school she runs – Manor's Hall Riding School, are stealing all my customers. She won't rest until she sees me ruined, but we'll show her, won't we?"

Jo and I nodded. It was a familiar story to us. Janey despised Angelica Kent who was the wealthy owner of a riding school well known for its professionalism and expertise. Every failure Janey had, she managed to attribute to Angelica. Theirs was a fierce and long running rivalry born from some trouble we did not fully understand. It involved me and my friends in that we had come to actively dislike anyone who went to Manor's Hall and naturally enough they disliked us. I suppose it added spice to our otherwise pretty mundane lives and at the time I though it was all very harmless.

"The whole gang will help," said Jo loyally. "We'll show them!"

Janey smiled. "You're good kids and I know that together we'll break her. We'll do it by fair means or foul."

We nodded, though I wasn't quite sure I liked the sound of Janey's venomous words. They seemed to embrace a little too much threat.

"Anyway Janey," said Jo brightly, changing the subject. "Luce will be getting her own pony in the next few days so you'll have another livery at the stables. That'll help, won't it?"

Janey beamed at this idea. She squeezed my arm in her bony grip "Your father is a shrewd man, Lucy," she said. "He's given me full instructions, I'm to choose you the ideal horse. You're a very lucky girl. I'm going to pick out a horse that will do us both proud, something that will show Angelica Kent she's not the only one who can keep blood stock!"

Jo nudged me playfully. "Oh, we've saved you the trouble. We've already found our ideal pony."

I didn't know what Jo was on about but she winked when she glanced at me and so I guessed she was about to pull Janey's leg.

"Lucy's fallen in love with him and no other pony will do for her. You do know about Elspeth Montgomery's mare having a foal don't you? Well, Luce plans to buy her foal and we're going to bring him up."

I giggled at this absurd suggestion, but to my surprise Janey's expression had visibly altered. She was furious. As Jo prattled on, I watched Janey with a growing sense of unease and confusion.

"Shut up!" she suddenly yelled at Jo, who stopped dead in mid-sentence. "You're a pair of spoilt brats who think all you have to say is I want this or I want that and sure enough you'll get it! Well, I'm not running a kindergarten for you or your foals, so think again!"

There was no point in even trying to reply to Janey. She was flushed with temper and more like a fire in full blaze than a normal person. Jo and I just watched dumbly as she staggered to her feet.

She leant down and roared, "I'm a sick woman with vultures on every side of me, wanting money, wanting

10

to see me ruined, and you two think life is one big joke, don't you? Well, I'll ring your father, Lucy. I'll tell him what an idiotic child he has and I'll tell him just what I think about your wretched foal too. That's what I'll do!"

As Janey straightened up she staggered and had to steady herself against the straw bales before storming out of the barn.

Jo's face had lost some of its colour, as I imagine mine had.

"What did I say?" Jo murmured. "Or has she flipped?"

"I have no idea but it wasn't one of your better jokes," I sneered. "She's going to ring my Dad!"

"I don't understand it Luce. She'd get the same amount of livery money for a foal as she would for a horse. What does it matter to her?"

I shook my head. Janey was a temperamental woman but I'd never seen her act so violently over something so outwardly unimportant. It was a mystery. Then, suddenly I saw something half concealed in the flattened straw where Janey had been lying. I scrambled forward and dug it out. It was a bottle, almost empty and it was whisky.

"She never had a dizzy spell at all," whispered Jo urgently. "She was drunk!"

In the same place, there was a crumpled sheet of headed paper with typing on it. With growing excitement Jo and I huddled over it. Above us, the rain hammered deadingly as we read:

Dear Madam,
   Our client Mr Nailer of Drew House Farm has informed us that, despite repeated demands, his bill

11

of March 1st for £1,000 remains outstanding. We are therefore instructed to inform you that if this amount is not paid in full within the next month, legal proceedings will be instituted.

Yours,
John Bulman
On behalf of Jennings, Baldwin and Stubbs, Solicitors.

When Jo and I left the haybarn I had a strange, fleeting premonition about the summer that lay ahead. Janey Squires had her problems but it passed briefly through my mind that her troubles were going to affect me and even the new horse I was going to get. It seemed improbable, and I certainly didn't dwell on it, but it was a shadow that in time I would come to wish I had looked at closer.

Chapter Two
The Ideal Pony?

After we explained our joke, Janey snapped mysteriously out of her savage temper. She went as far as to apologise "It's my poor nerves," she said with a sob of melodramatic emotion. Her "nerves" were the result of pressure and the pressure was the result of Angelica Kent. Everything that ailed Janey Squires and Long Meadows Riding School could be traced back to Angelica Kent. She sat on the bench in the stables and complained about the cruel injustice of life and how she wished Manor's Hall could meet with some disaster. Jo and I made allowances for her. Having seen the solicitor's letter and the empty bottle we knew she wasn't quite herself. When Janey had temporarily exhausted her supply of temper and bitterness she announced that she was going home to lie down. Quite honestly, we were relieved to see her go.

Shortly after Janey had left, the gang arrived. Jo and I were in the tackroom trying to get a fire started. If I had to choose one part of Long Meadows Riding School that I could have kept as my own, it would be that unobtrusive little tackroom. It was cosy and warm and it belonged to us kids. There was no tack kept in it. Instead, there were two armchairs, a sofa, a table and a small cooker. Janey came in occasionally but it was predominantly our territory where we met, cooked, laughed and talked. As everyone barged in and sprawled around the room, they asked the inevitable question "Where was Janey?" I'd hectored Jo not to tell anyone else about finding the bottle and the letter. I felt sorry for Janey. Jo was harder about such things but when she told the gang what had happened, she neatly left out our find. As she talked, I glanced at the attentive faces of our audience. Kay Davenport was seated in the best armchair. She was fifteen, and a bully. She could be understanding or she could be cruel. She could act sensibly and grown up or she could act like someone just out of kindergarten. I always tried to steer a wide course around her whenever possible. Kay's best friend and side kick was Dee who had puppy dog eyes and dark lank hair. If Kay was the born leader, and she was, Dee was the follower. Dee could be charm itself if she wanted something but underneath it she was two faced and as slippery as an eel.

Paul Anthony Wayne Nicholson (Pawn for short) was sitting in the corner. He was a great looking blond kid, a year younger than I was. He was seriously in love with Jo but she wasn't interested in him, saying he was too young. Nothing deterred him though, and he trailed after us as loyal as a dog. Arabella Box was fourteen. She was pretty and clever. If she'd ever chosen to, she could have toppled Kay from her position of power but sadly Arab was far too easy going for confrontation. The youngest of us was Michelle. She was ten and the tag-along. I suppose, all in all, we were a funny bunch but up until that summer we had mostly got on very well together. Kay's bullying usually found its outlet with anyone from Manor's

14

Hall. As long as you were on the inside with the gang, you were safe, and Jo and I were.

We spent the morning ignoring any work that ought to have been done and lazing in the tackroom. Janey's rivalry with Angelica was the main topic of conversation. We speculated wildly about the ins and outs of their competitiveness and, of course, the outcome. At first glance it looked clear cut. Angelica Kent was very rich and successful, her riding school was much bigger and better equipped than Long Meadows. She was the District Commissionaire of the Pony Club and a local big-wig in every way. Janey, on the other hand, was more like a social leper. Her riding school was in desperate need of improvement and she scorned the Pony Club and all it stood for. We weren't encouraged to mention it never mind join it. Lately, there'd been a steady stream of Janey's customers leaving to attend Manor's Hall and with six weeks of summer holidays ahead, the desk diary was peculiarly empty. There were, however, two things Janey had to her advantage. The first was that she was the only riding school in the area that took liveries. Strangely, Manor's Hall refused to. Kay and Arab both kept their own ponies at Long Meadows and I would do the same when my pony was bought. The second, and perhaps the more important, was that Janey was a fighter who didn't know the meaning of "giving up". I liked that about her.

It was lunch-time when our conversation was interrupted. We hadn't even noticed that the rain had stopped and that the sun was beginning to shine. It took Mo Mogaran – Janey's only adult friend and part-time helper, to burst in on our excited chatter and thereby bring it to an abrupt end. She didn't look in a very friendly mood.

"Is Janey alright?" asked Arab, neatly intercepting Mo's obvious intention to bawl us out for skiving.

"She's much better," Mo replied dismissively. She glanced unsmilingly round the room at each of us.

"I've never known her go home before," said Kay. "I mean she's always ill but she never goes home, does she?"

Mo lit a cigarette with slow icy disregard for Kay's comments. She inhaled a breath before fixing Kay with a hard stare. "Have you spent the whole morning here – speculating about Janey's health?"

"Well, it has been thundering," replied Kay uneasily.

"It's stopped," said Mo. "I presume the horses have all been mucked out and exercised?"

This was met by silence. Kay shuffled uncomfortably before saying, "We'll do it now."

We began to file quickly out of the tackroom. Mo Mogaran was tough and hers wasn't the kind of toughness you questioned. As we were leaving she asked me to wait. "Would it be all right if Janey and I took you to see a horse for sale, this evening?"

I swallowed my surprise and nodded excitedly. "Has Janey spotted a good one?" I asked. "She never mentioned it to me this morning."

Mo stared into the low dying fire. She pushed a hand through her short, fashionable hair before replying. It seemed a weary gesture. "Someone has just called her about a horse they think might be suitable."

"How big? What colour?"

"I don't have the details, Luce," she replied, still

16

gazing at the fire. "You'll have to wait until you see him."

"Brilliant," I enthused. "The others can come with us, can't they?"

She nodded and as I turned towards the door she suddenly said sharply, "Lucy."

I looked expectantly at her.

"Just don't get too excited," she muttered. "He may not be the right horse for you. OK?"

"OK," I shrugged but I couldn't stop myself from adding, "I think he will be, Mo. I have a feeling about him."

That evening we all duly squashed into Janey's untaxed calamity of a van and set off for the dealer's yard. Mo drove and Janey sat beside her looking tired and tense. In the back the gang fooled on and sang noisy, out of tune pop songs. But I didn't join in, my mind was on other things.

"Don't you know anything about this pony, Janey?" I yelled over the noise.

"I do know he's a bit bigger than we'd expected," shouted Janey, with a little cough. "He's about fifteen two."

"That's all right," put in Kay. "My horse Max, is fifteen hands and Lucy's almost as tall as me."

"Lucy's a tall girl for her age," agreed Janey seriously, which set Jo and Pawn off into a sprawl of laughter.

"You'd grow out of a pony in no time. It's far better we buy a decent sized horse," she added.

I shrugged. "I don't mind him being big." I was getting keener by the minute to see the horse. When we drove into a huge, housing estate, I thought Mo had taken a wrong turn.

"You can't keep horses here. There're no fields," said Arab, but Mo said she'd heard of Fred Mannering, the dealer, and knew where he lived. We eventually came to a stuttering halt outside a very ordinary looking house. It didn't seem to have even the vaguest connection with anything equestrian and I was puzzled.

We filed up the garden path with Jo and Chelle in fits of giggles, and Pawn saying, "Perhaps they keep the horse in the kitchen." Janey, who was dressed in her very best riding clothes, was not amused. As usual, when in public, she was hysterically keen to give exactly the right impression. She always emphasized it was *us* who let her down. "Shut up, the lot of you," she muttered. She had her back to the door and didn't see it open. When she turned she nearly jumped out of her skin, which set us off laughing again.

"Oh, hello. We've come to see the thoroughbred I believe you have for sale," said Janey in a voice she usually reserved for the telephone.

"Aye," retorted the woman in a terribly unimpressed tone. "Fred's out the back. Come through."

She led us through the house and into a large scruffy yard, in the corner of which were two loose boxes. It backed onto a large field, and coming through the open gate was a tough, heavily built man who was introduced to us as Fred Mannering. I was already feeling disappointed. I didn't like the look of anything I'd seen and least of all did I like the look of Fred Mannering with his unshaven chin and tattooed arms.

When I was pointed out to him as the prospective buyer, his small eyes scrutinized me with a special and lingering interest. Then he shouted to a youth

18

who was lounging nearby. "Bring out the thoroughbred."

Jo dug her elbow into me as the anticipation mounted. A huge bay horse was led into the yard. He was thin and tired and walked with a long slow stride. We all rushed forward to stroke and pet him, but he laid back his ears and threw his head nervously away.

"All thoroughbreds are nervy," laughed Janey confidently. "It's their breeding."

"He's much bigger than fifteen two," I said, in awe of the size of the horse.

Janey was very dismissive. "Oh well, give or take a few inches."

The horse was as still as a statue as he was saddled. The others stood further back but I stroked his bowed neck and felt immediately very sorry for him. I was taking no notice of the lad who was fastening the girths, but as he leant down he whispered urgently, "This poor sod's going to be shot tomorrow if you don't buy him."

"What?" I exclaimed.

"Shh. It's true," he murmured. "Fred's a cruel pig and he took a fall from this one two days ago. If you don't take him away from here, he's going to the knacker's yard tomorrow afternoon."

"I don't believe you," I said, but then I added more uncertainly, "Is the horse dangerous, then?"

The lad shook his head, but before he could say anything, Fred Mannering joined us. My mind buzzed as Fred gave me his salesman patter about the horse being an ex-steeplechaser who'd won his last race.

I was legged on in a daze. I kicked my feet into the stirrups, half wondering what to expect. The horse didn't move a muscle. I gently urged him forward and rode into the paddock with Janey crying, "Oh, don't they suit each other?"

I walked him up the length of the field, cantered him on the corner and walked him back to join the others. He was a very bouncy ride, but surprisingly manageable.

"He's got a lovely action, Lucy," said Janey encouragingly. "He went so well. Did you like him?"

I said I did and dismounted. We walked back to the yard and I was able to tell Jo and the gang what the lad had told me. It caused a predictable outburst of fury towards Fred Mannering and extreme sympathy for the poor doomed racehorse.

"You must save him, Luce," cried Jo passionately. "We can't leave here tonight knowing the poor animal's going to die. We just can't!"

Everyone agreed with her and as an unsuspecting Fred stood a little way apart, we whispered the story to Janey and Mo. Janey wasn't in the least surprised. She told us in a hushed voice that things like this were very common in the dark and dingy underworld of horse dealing. I thought I heard Mo groan, but I couldn't be sure. I could have done with her advice, but it wasn't forthcoming. In fact, she was unusually quiet and withdrawn. I stroked the horse again. Frankly, he was not my idea of the ideal pony. He was at least sixteen two and he was a racehorse. But as I stood next to him trying to fathom out what to do, he poked his nose into my hand and pushed it around for a moment before resting it there. His eyes were as sad as I'd ever seen. I reckoned he needed me far more than I needed him, but my mind was made up. I looked at Mr Mannering. "I'll have him," I announced.

"Oh good," shouted Janey. "He's a beautiful animal. You won't regret it."

Both Mr Mannering and Janey seemed elated about my decision. There was a great deal of celebratory hand shaking and back slapping being done. Meanwhile the huge stringy racehorse and I stared at one another and I wondered what I'd done.

Chapter Three
The Challenge Cup

I never actually told my mum and dad the exact details of my new horse. I called him a "biggish pony". They were both basking in complete ignorance where horses were concerned and they thought he sounded "ideal". I suppose they had other things on their minds. They'd spent most of that year arguing bitterly and blaming each other for anything and everything. It was one of the reasons I was going to boarding school that autumn – "for my own good". It didn't seem so good to me. I liked the friends I had and I didn't particularly want any new ones. It was a time of change and through it I clung to the old reliables, Jo and the gang, Long Meadows and now my new horse. They at least, would never change, or so I naively believed that fresh July morning as I made my way to Jo's house.

It turned out that Jo had stayed up late the night before to watch a movie and as a result she was having enormous difficulties in waking up. It meant we were late to Long Meadows. The gang and Janey would normally have been rushing about doing the many things that needed doing, but they weren't. Instead, they were "in conference" in the tackroom and when we entered, Janey leapt to her feet as if she hadn't seen me for a year.

"Lucy, come and sit down. We've got some wonderful news for you."

I squashed in between Kay and Dee on the sofa and Jo sat on the arm of the chair.

"We are going to enter for this year's Challenge Cup," announced Janey with almost majestic pride. If she'd said she was going to swim the Channel I couldn't have been more surprised. This was after all a woman who'd brought us up on a diet of anti-competition!

"The Challenge Cup," I replied dizzily. "But Manor's Hall always win it and you said you wouldn't be seen dead competing with them. You said . . ."

"I know what I said, Lucy," interrupted Janey sharply. "But things have changed slightly. I feel that it's time we showed our true colours."

"But you hate competitions," said Jo. "And isn't the Challenge Cup organised by the Pony Club?"

Janey's face set slightly as she glared at Jo. "What's wrong with you two? A little competition never hurt anyone."

"You said it did," muttered Jo huffily. "You said . . ."

"Stop telling me what I've said," hissed Janey. "You've obviously both misunderstood me. Don't you want to beat Manor's Hall at their own game? Don't you want to see us triumph over *that* woman?"

Jo glanced at me and I nodded quite eagerly, then asked innocently, "But how could we?"

"Well, Lucy dear," said Janey with bloodcurdling sweetness, "I think you're an absolute must for our little team."

"Me?" I gasped. "Oh no. I don't know what this horse of mine will be like. I think I should get used to him first, before entering him for a point to point race."

"Nonsense," said Janey. "He's a steeplechaser isn't he? That's what he's trained for – jumping over fences!"

"Yes, but with me on him?" I asked uncertainly.

"Of course," hooted Janey. "Kay can ride Max and you can ride your race-horse. That's settled. Just sign this entry form."

Janey was moving so fast that she was leaving me behind. The entry form and pen were shoved into my hands while Janey padded around the room seemingly fit to burst with impatience and nerves. I glanced down the printed page noticing my details were all filled in apart from the name of my horse and my signature. I wrote Sun-Dance where the horse's name was to go.

"Shouldn't I be in the under fourteen's race and not the open, Janey?" I asked.

She replied with a short hysterical laugh. "Don't be so soft! You're going to be riding a fine thoroughbred. You'd be the laughing stock if you entered the kiddies' race."

I shrugged. I was undecided. I'd heard enough about The Challenge Cup to know it was a tough race and it was usually entered by serious riders. I even thought I remembered that this year there was some prize money on offer. On the other hand, it was a Pony Club event for young people, although not normally as young as twelve. Janey was tapping her foot impatiently. "Well. Hurry up," she urged. "You do want to help us, don't you?"

"Yes, but . . ."

"Oh, go on, Lucy," yawned Arab, and the others echoed her sentiments.

"It would be great if we could win the cup,"said Jo encouragingly.

I picked up the pen, signed my name with a flourish and, believe me, it wasn't long before I bitterly regretted it.

My horse, Sun-Dance, arrived at four o'clock that afternoon. It took ten of us thirty minutes just to get him out of the horse box. He kicked Dee, came within quarter of an inch of savaging Michelle and had the horse-box driver scared half to death.

"Isn't he playful?" commented Janey, but I noticed she hurried off with vague excuses of work to be done.

Sun-Dance wasn't playful. He was about as wild as the west wind. There was no misinterpreting the signs. He'd lost that tired, tranquilized look of the day before and in its place was a surge of electricity that flowed through him as if he had power lines for muscles. Now he really did look the part of a thoroughbred racehorse and now I had a good idea of just what it meant to own him.

Kay accurately read my silent misgivings. "When will we see you on him, Luce?" she asked snidely.

"Not today," I said. "I have to go home – early!"

Kay smiled in such a satisfied way that it endorsed my suspicion that she was jealous. Janey had been heaping attention on me lately and Kay didn't like it. To make matters worse, Janey had entered the two of us for 'The Challenge Cup' whilst making it quite clear that she thought I was the only one with any chance of winning it. I ignored the slight tension that had followed Kay's sneering smile and walked away.

"You'll have to ride him tomorrow," said Pawn, as

we trailed out of the stables. "Or they'll think you're scared."

"I know that," I snapped irritably.

The next morning was the first really hot day of the summer. The sky was clear blue and the fields were so fresh they looked as if someone had glossed paint over them. Everything on the outside seemed perfect but I was worried. I wasn't relishing the thought of riding my racehorse in front of the others. I couldn't make out why he was so different from when I'd seen him at Mannering's yard but there was no mistaking that he was. Jo thought it was the journey that had upset him. "I bet he's different again today," she said confidently as we walked into the yard at Long Meadows. I hoped she was right but she wasn't. Sun-Dance was worse than ever, and Kay Davenport was loving every second of it.

"So you'll be riding him in the paddock after lunch," she said while her eyes pierced me for any flicker of fear I might show. "That will be worth watching. I bet he's fast, Luce. I bet he goes like a launched missile when he goes."

By one o'clock that afternoon the atmosphere at Long Meadows was one of intense nervous excitement. Somehow, we got Dance saddled. He lunged and tried to bite, but we stuck with it and eventually we managed. When he was led to the yard, I could only gaze at him with a sick feeling in the pit of my stomach. An inner fire seemed to have flared in him. He pawed the ground testily and tried to back away. His taut nerves clearly indicated to me that this was one dangerous horse.

"I don't think I'll watch," said Michelle. "I don't like the sight of blood."

I ran my damp hand down his neck. "Steady, Dance," I whispered, as I pulled the stirrup down. Someone legged me into the saddle which he didn't like one bit. He flung his head around and swung his hindquarters. Even the gang had fallen into an awed silence, only Janey's high pitched voice reached me.

"You're going to have to show him you're the boss. He's a little fresh and he might have it in his mind to test you out."

We'd gone three paces and I knew Dance had already tested me and found me sadly lacking. Waves of dread began to wash over me as we bulldozed our way to the paddock at the back of the stables. Jo and Kay both had hold of his bridle but it was like trying to hold back a juggernaut. The gate to the paddock was pulled open and Dance, seeing a great deal of fun and adventure ahead, rushed blindly into the open field. Kay was knocked against the gate post, but Jo hung on.

"Don't let go," I cried to her as Dance bucked like a rodeo horse. He ducked his head and rammed it into her but at that critical moment, Mo Mogaran stepped forward and grasped hold of the bridle. She must have only just arrived because it was the first I'd seen of her all that day.

"Get off him," she said to me, and gladly I kicked my feet free of the stirrups and dismounted. I was no coward but I wasn't up to riding Dance. "Get my hard hat from the stables," Mo said. If she'd asked me to go to London and get the Crown Jewels I'd have tried. I was immeasurably grateful to her. I returned. She pushed the hat firmly down on her head and taking the reins in one hand got lightly into the saddle. Dance started his antics again but Mo was a whole different ball game to me, and they looked quite evenly matched as they fought for dominance that hot afternoon. I'd always skirted wide of Mo Mogaran, but on that first day with Dance she won my friendship and respect outright.

"Haven't you all got something better to do than watch me?" she shouted to everyone. "Buzz off, the lot of you, except for Lucy." The gang and even Janey, bowed to Mo's demand. They wandered disconsolately back to the stables while I stayed to watch the first round of what was to prove quite a fight.

Chapter Four
Where Respect is Due

"When I was your age, Lucy," said Janey Squires, leaning on a pitchfork, "I was riding thoroughbreds, polo ponies, top showjumpers. I never knew fear, not a flicker of it. I was a natural."

"I'd love to see you ride Dance," said Jo, winking at me.

Janey took the cigarette from her mouth and tapped the ash from it. "If only I could," she said.

"Why can't you?" asked Pawn.

"Because I'm under the doctor," retorted Janey. "I'm a sick woman."

It was an odd fact about Janey Squires, but we'd never seen her ride a horse. Each time a new pupil arrived, which was rarely, Janey would reel off the same introductory speech. It was probably best described as a synopsis of the noble art of equitation and she recited it with a theatrical flourish. It was left to us to actually teach the lessons but Janey made sure to miss *that* small fact out of her introductory speech. Most parents were taken in by it and happily left their kids to our amateurish devices. Believe me, it was a case of the partially sighted leading the blind! I had heard it rumoured that Janey couldn't ride that she'd just learnt hefty chunks of theory from a book but I liked to think she could. Those of us who were loyal to Janey preferred the idea that she'd had a bad fall which had tragically ended her glorious riding career. Anyway, I knew she would never ride Dance and as I thought of this my mind turned automatically to Mo Mogaran.

"Mo was brilliant when she rode Dance," I said enthusiastically. "She's the best rider I've ever seen."

"Mo's all right," replied Janey dismissively. "She's what I'd call self-taught. She's never picked up the finer nuances of horsemanship." Janey tittered at this with her hand over her mouth which set Kay and Dee off laughing. It annoyed me. I hated the way Janey put people down behind their backs. She was always doing it about Mo. Normally I didn't say anything, but that day I flared up in her defence.

"No one else would have ridden him. You'd all have stood around gawping while I broke my neck. Mo was brilliant. She could actually control him."

"Oh, she's a very strong woman. I'll give her that," replied Janey with an annoying little smile.

"She's more like a man than a woman," howled Kay in an outburst of nastiness that she wouldn't have dared to exhibit if Mo had been anywhere near.

It was more than I could take. I jumped impulsively to my feet. "She's worth ten of you," I snapped to Kay. "At least she's got guts. You're all talk and no action."

I stormed out of the barn feeling angry and confused. It was a week since Mo had first ridden Dance and since then I'd spent a great deal of time in her company. We'd worked hard to improve Dance and I liked Mo. She was really trying to get to grips with Dance, something I didn't have a hope of doing. He wasn't an easy horse for either of us. His nerves and

30

iron will led Mo to think he'd probably been ill treated.

"Hey, are you off your head or what?" asked Jo as she joined me. "Kay didn't like what you said to her just now."

"Tough," I grunted.

"Kay's alright if you stay on the right side of her, but you don't want her as an enemy."

"Tell her that, Jo, not me. She's the one who always comes out with the snide wisecracks."

"I know. I know," shrugged Jo understandingly. "But can't you just let her be? Stop getting her mad, Luce. She's got it in for you. When you walked out of the barn, she immediately suggested we build a cross country course in the paddock so that you and she can get some practice in before The Challenge Cup. Janey's agreed!"

"But I can't jump Dance over a cross country course," I exclaimed. "I can't do anything with him at all."

"Kay knows that and she knows only too well that Janey's gone quite potty over this Challenge Cup business. I'd hate to be you if you decide to tell her you're not going to enter it."

"But that's not being very fair to me, is it?" I said. "I should have a say in it – he's my horse, it's my decision."

Jo put her hand on my shoulder and her voice dropped almost to a whisper as she said, "But don't you think Janey's gone kind of strange this summer? She's not acting normal. She's got it into her head that you winning The Challenge Cup is somehow going to save Long Meadows. I wouldn't disappoint her, Luce, not at this stage anyway. God knows what she'd do."

31

I thought about what Jo had said for the rest of that day. It was certainly true that Janey was more fired up than we'd ever seen her before. She wanted that Challenge Cup like a drowning man wants saving. She thought I could get it for her and she wouldn't listen to reason. If I broached the subject of Dance being difficult, she was always dismissive, saying all thoroughbreds were difficult. She was also building me up in front of the others. Kay didn't like it, but Michelle almost had a crush on me! It was strange for me, I was no better a rider than Jo and Arab, but Janey kept making out I was a young Pat Smythe and Dance was my Prince Hal. I suppose some of it was going to my head because occasionally I found myself daydreaming about winning The Challenge Cup. Then, I'd come back to reality and remember I hadn't even been off the lunge rein yet. The building of the cross country course that afternoon brought the problem home to me with resounding clarity. It was as a result of that I decided to broach the whole subject of Dance with my father.

"Dance is very spirited," I said, over tea that evening.

"Good," nodded my dad.

I tried again. "Mo Mogaran thinks he's too spirited."

Dad looked up. "I thought the riding school was run by Janey Squires. Surely she's the real judge of whether the horse is too spirited or not?"

"Janey's the boss," I said, "but Mo has been helping me with Dance and he's turning out to be more difficult than we'd thought he would."

"I hope you don't mean he's no good, Lucy. He damn well cost enough."

"Did he?" I asked with some surprise.

"If the horse is dangerous," interrupted my mother, "then I don't want Lucy riding him."

"He's not dangerous," I said. "Just spirited." But I was wasting my breath. My father was glaring at my mother.

"I trusted Janey Squires to buy a suitable pony for my twelve year old daughter. If she can't do that simple task she must be some kind of fool," exclaimed my father excitedly.

"From what I've heard, she is," shouted my mother. "She could be a con-artist, David. I said at the time you ought to have gone along to see the horse, but, oh no, you had a more important business engagement."

"And where were you at the time?" roared my dad.

I leapt up and shouted, "I love him!"

Both my parents stared silently at me.

"I love Dance," I said steadily. "He's the best horse in the world and I don't want to sell him, so you can stop arguing, can't you?"

The following afternoon was like "D" day for me. The cross country course had been duly erected and Kay was madly enthusiastic to see me ride it. I'd shared my fears with Jo. I didn't like feeling scared of Dance and I didn't want the others to know. I thought they'd probably laugh and I didn't want to fall out with the gang that summer. I wanted things to run smoothly because they weren't really running smoothly anywhere else in my life. I had a big dread of being the one who was left out and getting talked about all the time. I planned to fake courage but it didn't work out like that.

When Dance was led out, I watched him whipping around the yard and I knew I couldn't ride him.

Janey's comments were inane. "What a lovely horse he is," she said as he lashed out with a hind-leg. "So full of spirit and energy, a certain winner."

My heart was pounding. My mouth was going dry. I had to speak up otherwise it would be too late.

"I don't think I will ride him this afternoon," I said tentatively.

All eyes turned on me until I felt I was in a blinding spotlight. I was hot and red but I stayed determined. Kay smiled sourly. "Are you frightened, Lucy?" she asked with a callous bluntness.

I met her eyes with difficulty. "Yes, I am."

"Oh for goodness sake!" exclaimed Janey selfishly. Her infamous temper was rapidly rising to boiling point. I grabbed Dance's reins before anyone could say anything else and led him back into the stables. Once inside I flung off his tack furiously. I hated myself and tears of anger stung my eyes.

I turned on Dance but unexpectedly he nuzzled my ear, catching one of my tears on his nose. He stretched his long neck towards the roof and showed his teeth as if he was laughing at me for being afraid of him. It was the first gentleness he'd shown since arriving at Long Meadows and my initial instinctive thoughts of selling him, there and then began to recede. I stroked his neck and realized that if I was being truly sensible and logical then I would sell him, because he was too big and too strong. I wasn't very sensible. I was romantic, my heart invariably shooting out to renegade animals like Dance. Anyhow if Dance was capable of being this friendly he was surely capable of being ridden by me. Fired by this fresh determination I plucked up the courage to face the others, finding them sitting morosely around the desk. Their moods were muted and Janey's prompting glance at Kay was not lost on me.

"Look, Lucy, we all understand how you must feel," bleated Kay. "And I'm sorry if I've been pestering you to jump him, but I'm just so keen for you to do well on Dance."

She was lying. Her words were altogether too soft, her face too hard.

Janey echoed her sentiments. "He's such a good horse and you're such a promising rider. You'll make a winning team, I know it."

I was glad they were being at least outwardly nice, but at that moment the door of the stables opened and Mo came in. She asked what was going on so Kay began to tell her. Only Kay kept using words like "scared" and "couldn't manage". Mo glanced at me but I just looked away, deadly embarrassed. When at last Kay was satisfied she'd done full justice to the tale I wished the ground would open up and swallow me.

Mo said, "That's not what I call being scared. I wouldn't jump Dance today either. I'm not such a fool as that, neither's Lucy. He's not ready, and we're not ready. We're bringing him on gently and it maddens me to think of your interference."

Kay looked at her feet as Mo continued. "Would you jump him, Kay?"

The silence was deafening. I was beginning to enjoy it.

"No, I didn't think so," continued Mo.

"He's a very good horse," interrupted Janey.

"He's too big for Lucy," retorted Mo blackly.

"Don't start saying that now!" exclaimed Janey,

jumping to her feet. "I can't recall you saying it at the time we bought him."

They faced each other with such obvious animosity that it left me bewildered.

"Which is why I'm helping out now," said Mo with a curled lip. "I think we both owe Lucy that much."

I had no idea what they were talking about, but Mo's words had silenced a very voluble Janey. As she sat back down and fumbled for her cigarettes, Mo said to me, "C'mon, we'll put Dance on the lunge rein and continue where we left off yesterday, unless Kay changes her mind and wants to show us what she can do on him . . ."

I couldn't help smiling, but Kay blushed deeply, which seemed to give Mo Mogaran great satisfaction.

Chapter Five

The Race

Kay's resentment of me deepened considerably over the next few hectic days. She never missed an opportunity to express confidently that it was she who had the only real chance in The Challenge Cup. After all, I was a mere beginner in comparison and barely off the lead rein! She was naturally careful that Mo didn't hear her. Jo had warned me about finding myself at loggerheads with Kay but the tension between us had just roller coasted without any help from me. Her insults made me indignant and reckless to prove her wrong.

It was a damp, chilly morning when Mo and I were working hard with Dance. I was riding him but as usual it was on the lunge rein. He had improved a little but he was, as always, temperamental and especially bored with the schooling this particular day. At last Mo unclipped the long rein and suggested she gave him a gallop. I dismounted, feeling slightly huffy over not being able to gallop on my own horse, even though I knew she was right.

"I might try him over those jumps after you?" I said with the outward appearance of calm self-assurance.

"Don't be daft," replied Mo, with a bluntness she was well known for and not always liked for.

"I can manage him," I lied. "He's come on a lot over these last few days."

"Janey's obviously stuffing him with corn," said Mo. "I'm going to speak to her about it. He's far too lively for you this morning. Don't tell me Kay's still winding you up about riding him?"

"She thinks I'm soft," I shrugged.

"Let her think what she likes. He's a sixteen two, ex-steeplechaser, not a ride at the funfair. I wish you'd get that into your head once and for all."

"I am trying to," I said.

"Good," nodded Mo emphatically, and without another word she swung Dance away. I climbed onto the five bar gate to sit and watch. Dance was quick to start playing out his rodeo horse fantasy. Mo was equally quick to put an end to it. They argued with each other for a few minutes until Dance only niggled on with a few ill-mannered bucks. Mo was laughing at him. She shouted across to me that she thought she'd let him have some of his own way, then she set him at the low fence we'd recently erected. He went towards it with fierce acceleration, jumped beautifully and pulled hard to gallop when he landed. Mo leant into his neck and he stretched himself out, at once producing a terrific burst of speed and power. His big stride ate up the ground until you'd have thought he was in an actual race. As they approached the top corner, Mo tried to steady him. Dance didn't want to be steadied. He was enjoying himself. Mo persisted with all her strength but he was stronger. They shot into that top corner all wrongly. We'd set up a jump there and Dance blazed towards it. I was on my feet even before the accident occurred. I saw Dance cat leap, thump the top of it and pitch onto his knees.

Mo was tossed aside like a rag doll. Dance was up in an instant, but Mo lay horribly still. I covered the distance between us in seconds until, panting, I dropped down beside her. She was clearly in great pain. Her eyes were open but her face was pale and set. Her arm was twisted awkwardly under her and she couldn't free it. I knew better than to touch her. I tore back down the length of the paddock to the stables where Kay dialled 999 for an ambulance. The rest of us hurried back to Mo. It was the worst wait I've ever known, the sky was dark and the rain began to drizzle down on us. Janey, for once was in control, and certainly calmer than I was. I kept staring across to where Dance was standing with his snapped reins trailing. Mo seemed to read my very thoughts.

"Dance slipped," she explained from between clenched teeth. "It was more my fault, check he's alright, Luce."

Reluctantly I left her side. Dance was trembling but he wasn't hurt. I was annoyed with him. I thought it was his fault but he seemed so sad and sorry standing there in the rain yet glad I'd come across to him. He kept nuzzling me as if to say I didn't mean this to happen and in my heart I believed that he didn't.

At last the ambulance came speeding up the narrow lane, its blue lights flashing ominously and with nerve snapping urgency. The ambulance men were reassuring and they joked carelessly with Mo but all the time her face told another story. Within minutes they'd sped away leaving me by the side of the lane watching the blue light until it was out of sight. Then I went and sat down next to Jo on the mounting block. I couldn't help but ask myself how dangerous Dance

39

was? Had he been running away with Mo? If he could do that with her, what chance had I?

"Oh dear, what a mess!" commented Kay coldly. "We won't be seeing much more of Mo this summer. I'm just wondering, Luce, who on earth's going to ride Dance for you now?" I glanced up to meet her smooth sardonic face, and all my misgivings about Dance and my own ability seemed to rise up in me, but I fought them back down and said quietly, "I am."

Kay smiled. We both knew I had to mean it, otherwise time would make a nonsense of my brave words. I suppose that was why Kay appeared so pleased with life for the rest of that awful day. She didn't think I could take over where Mo had left off, and I had a feeling she'd just bide her time until she could prove it to everyone else.

We got the news eventually, Mo's elbow was broken. It would be months before she rode again. It was a devastating blow to both me and Janey. Mo had been something of an anchor for Janey's unruly, out of control ship, and it was probably the worst moment to be without her. Janey needed someone to share her dizzy demands, but she need not have worried, Kay was quickly there. It was just the chance she'd been waiting for. She'd never liked Mo Mogaran. With her out of the way, Kay could lord it over us. Not that she was entirely tyrannical. She was too clever for that. In different circumstances perhaps even I would have followed Kay Davenport to the ends of the earth, but Dance and The Challenge Cup were between us that summer and she didn't intend to forget it.

I was worried about Dance. He wasn't getting enough hard exercise. I'd started to take him out with two of the gang coming along to lead him. It sounds soft but it was the only way we could control him. We took turns riding but we never went faster than a slow canter and most of the time we kept him at a walk. It was making Janey more hysterical than usual. She still had her sights fixed on The Challenge Cup. I'd really believed she would have seen sense, by now, what with Mo's accident and my obvious inexperience. But in the fiction Janey had weaved no facts emerged. She leant on Kay to put the problem right and each day I expected an aggressive confrontation with her but it didn't happen quite like that.

One afternoon, Jo, Chelle and I were out near the old disused railway track exercising Dance when Jo spotted Kay riding Max, and Dee on Flicka. I would have preferred to have ignored them but they waved across to us and cantered over. Immediately, Dance became very much harder to control.

"Dee and I are going to have a race along the railway line," announced Kay. "Are you going to join us, Luce?"

"No thanks."

Max was a fairly excitable horse at the best of times but Kay was making a point of reining him in too tightly which was making him edgy. Dance started to snort and paw the ground restlessly as if he'd understood that emotive word "race". I shortened my reins nervously.

"Dance will go mad," I said. "Wait until we get away before you start, Kay."

"I don't think I can," she laughed. "Look at old Max, he's dying to be off."

She was digging her heels into him and holding him

back at the same time. Dee began to do the same with Flicka.

"You've planned this," said Jo with a sneer. "Haven't you?"

Kay didn't need to reply. The answer was obvious. Dance's nerves were on fire. He suddenly shied, knocking Chelle over. Kay and Dee laughed.

"Go," shouted Kay.

They both shot forward and tore onto the open track. Dance gave Jo no chance to hold on to him. He reared and leapt into the air like Pegasus before breaking into a fast and furious gallop. I was almost unseated as we swerved through the gateway with all the sharp agility of a polo pony. Rapidly the lead they had over us began to look more like inches than metres. Dance's enormous stride pummelled the track until we flew past Flicka and Dee. I tugged weakly at the reins, gave up and clung to his mane instead. We were thundering down on Kay and Max like a greyhound chasing after a rabbit.

"Stop," I yelled. "Stop".

We splashed at a flat out gallop through the puddles as Dance hugged the inside of the track and brought us alongside Max. In one dizzy moment we'd passed them and nothing but the open track lay ahead. I prayed feverishly that he'd slow down now that we'd beaten the opposition but he was enjoying himself. His long stride did even out and I did find myself at last in some sort of balance with it. Then the track opened into a kind of fenced coral and Dance's pace had to slow down. I shortened the hopelessly slack reins and pulled. He stopped dead, bucked once and I toppled over his head and landed with a bump on the ground. He snorted indignantly as he stood over me, then he roughly nudged the top of my hat as if to say, "Well, you didn't do too badly," and calmly sauntered away. I couldn't believe I was still alive. My legs were like jelly but I felt a strange glow of elation at having won. I didn't want Kay or Dee to know I'd fallen off so I caught Dance quickly. There wasn't a moment to lose as they were already clattering around the bend of the track. Dance had a very superior look on his face and I made an effort to match his happy arrogance.

"Hell, he's fast!" shouted Kay. "Are you all right? Did you fall off?"

"I dismounted," I lied.

"I've never seen anything like that," gabbled Dee. "I thought you were a goner."

It wasn't very long before Jo and Chelle added their voices to the chorus. Chelle was especially impressed. "You were sheer brill," she enthused. "Weren't you scared?"

I hesitated warily before replying, I wondered if Kay had heard me shout but she showed no signs that she had. I don't know exactly why I lied over something which would in time have to be proved again. I suppose I was drunk on the moment and not thinking logically.

"I wasn't scared," I said. "I told you, Kay, I was going to ride him. I just didn't want to be rushed into it."

When Kay and Dee rode off to finish their ride we headed back to Long Meadows flushed with our triumph. Jo and Chelle recounted an exaggerated version of the race, and tears sprung to Janey's eyes as she flung her arms round me. I hadn't expected quite so much fuss and it made me think uneasily that I'd been a bit hasty in my bigheadedness.

Later that evening I said a fond goodnight to my mad racehorse. I had already grown to love him despite everything but he knew I was a fraud. I hadn't been able to stop him during the race. I'd hung onto his mane and even screamed, but thankfully no-one knew it, except for me and Dance that is.

Chapter Six
Secrets

"You certainly showed them," laughed Jo. "I knew Dance could win. Oh, we've put Kay in her place once and for all. You beat her fair square and handled Dance like a professional jockey. Everyone's dead impressed, Luce."

"Um."

Jo and I were struggling back to Long Meadows with a large bag of picked grass swinging between us. It was a hot sunny day and Janey had despatched everyone to various grassy corners of the countryside to pick grass. It was her latest idea in an economy drive that was sweeping Long Meadows. She said it was a good supplement to the horses' diet, but it was, more importantly, free of charge.

"I think you and Dance might even win that Challenge cup," continued Jo.

"Don't be dumb," I murmured. It made me uncomfortable to receive praise from Jo when I knew it was undeserved.

"Who's being dumb?" asked Jo gruffly. "How many other kids have their own real live racehorse?"

"Manor's Hall have fantastic horses. Anyway, what do you mean by calling him a real live racehorse? Of course he's real. Of course he's alive. I'd look kinda funny riding a dead horse, wouldn't I?"

"Touchy, aren't you?" asked Jo brightly and then she added more seriously, "Janey says if you can gallop him, you can jump him. I bet he can jump too."

"Janey's a fool," I said irritably.

"Of course she is," agreed Jo calmly. "But even I believe it. After all you have told everyone he was easy to control. You must be a better rider than Mo Mogaran!"

"Jo, listen to me. That race was a fluke. The truth is . . ."

My words were suddenly interrupted by someone yelling Jo's name rather frantically. She clambered onto the fence to see who it was while I kicked my feet in the dust and waited impatiently. I'd been cut off in mid-stream of a critical confession, namely that I was not Long Meadow's answer to Angelica Kent and Manor's Hall.

"It's Chelle. She's waving for me to go over to her. I'll go if you can manage that grass on your own."

I said I could, and Jo vaulted lightly over the fence and ran off. I hoisted the bag of grass onto my back and with deep feelings carried it the short distance to Long Meadows.

I'd loved seeing Kay's face when I'd beaten her and equally I loved being the heroine of the riding school but there wasn't much point if I couldn't live up to it, or could I? As I thought back to my race with Kay a slightly different story began to dawn on me. I told myself that Dance had been keen, not unstoppable. He'd pulled at the bit but then any horse would, given those conditions. Janey was determined that I should ride in The Challenge Cup and she was wholly convinced I could win. I had my doubts that I would win but I could see the advantage of playing the part of the person who was going to try to win.

I went into the cool empty stables to see Dance. I patted him and watched his awesomely huge, strong frame as he moved restlessly round his box. He was an enormous horse in comparison to the ponies I was used to. I vainly tried to convince myself that there were other less hazardous solutions to riding him in The Challenge Cup, but since I refused to sell him it only left one alternative and it was equally as hopeless. I could go to Janey Squires and calmly tell her I was withdrawing from the Challenge Cup race. That of course would be akin to lighting the blue touch paper of a particularly dangerous firework and not being able to stand well back. The gang, and even Jo, would be disappointed. We all wanted to swipe that prestigious silver cup from Angelica Kent. Somehow it had fallen to me to do it.

As I stroked Dance, I heard footsteps at the far end of the stables. At first I took no notice but then I recognized Mo's voice. I was just about to shoot along to see her when her clearly angry words reached me and made me stop dead in my tracks.

"Janey, you're going too far. Lucy could be killed riding a horse like Dance."

I pressed against the partitioning wall and listened with my heart drumming nervously.

"Why don't you look past your hatred of Angelica Kent?" Mo exclaimed loudly. "Drop this mad plan to enter Lucy in The Challenge Cup."

Janey laughed sourly. "Haven't you changed your tune? All of a sudden you're very sanctimonious. You seem to have conveniently forgotten your part in it. Fred Mannering was your contact not mine."

"Shut up Janey. The walls around this place have ears. I'm not proud of it, that's why I'm here today, trying to talk you into getting the kid out of this race."

"The horse is good enough," grunted Janey. "He's a bit more temperamental than we imagined but he's taken to Lucy. I think he's going to be a one woman horse."

"Yes, I agree but you can't seriously expect her to win The Challenge Cup on him. She'll more probably break her neck. She's little more than a novice."

"For goodness sake, Mo, stop worrying," said Janey soothingly. "Dance is an ex-steeplechaser . . ."

"Look at my arm," Mo interrupted emphatically.

"That must have been your fault," retorted Janey. "Not Dance's."

"You know it wasn't! We've been friends a long time, Janey, but I don't like what's going on here. I think this is the ideal time for me to take a little holiday. After all, I'm not going to be much help to you with only one good arm, am I?"

"Do as you please, Mo," said Janey, ill temperedly, but she still added, "Yes, leave me in my hour of need, everyone else has!"

Mo laughed. I heard footsteps, a crash of the door and then Janey followed her out. I was left alone, puzzled and somewhat indignant by the strength of Mo's convictions that I ought not to ride in The Challenge Cup. She'd called me "little more than a novice" which just wasn't true. I'd been riding for two whole years. I was very experienced. This was one of those rare times when I actually thought Janey was right. Mo was worrying too much, but that in itself seemed inexplicable. Mo was normally the calmer one of the two. I couldn't even begin to fathom out why she was blaming herself for my buying Dance. I knew Fred Mannering was her contact, she'd told us that much, but Dance was my choice – she hadn't hectored me into buying him. In fact she'd hardly spoken a word all through that evening!

When I repeated all I'd overheard to Jo, she suggested that Mo may have banged her head when she'd fallen from Dance. Jo said bangs on the head could cause people to see things differently. I was keen to accept this. I didn't want to believe that the sane, normal Mo would ever describe me as a mere novice!

"You'll show her how good you really are when you win The Challenge Cup in September," said Jo confidently and I tended to agree with her.

I became even more satisfied about my ability as a horsewoman when I rode Dance in the paddock that afternoon. He was the best he'd ever been. I purposely cantered him past the jump he'd fallen at and back to the gate where the gang and Janey cheered my efforts enthusiastically. Mo, who hadn't yet left for her holiday didn't join in the applause.

"He's a one woman horse," shouted Janey. "You've won him over beautifully, Lucy. I'm so proud!"

"Oh, it was nothing," I smiled waving my hand like the Queen does when she passes her admiring subjects.

I took Dance round the paddock for a second time and I went a little faster. As we approached the top corner he began to pull hard. His Herculean strength made me feel as weak as a baby. I was scared by it but then he steadied himself and we arrived successfully and safely back with the others. They hadn't noticed that I'd had difficulties with him. Janey was nearly hysterical with happiness, which was having a contagious effect on the gang. Compliments were flying my way like confetti. Only Kay and Mo remained reserved, and I'm afraid I tarred them both with the same brush and concluded they were jealous.

When we took Dance into the stables I noticed Mo watching me with a frown of disapproval. Janey was twittering on about what a marvellous rider I was and how me and Dance were poetry in motion to watch. I was petting Dance and thanking him for being good. He was one hundred percent my horse now. Only that morning he'd refused to be brought in from the paddock by anyone but me. He'd given all the others the runaround until I'd stepped in. It was the accumulation of all these things that created my conceit and my temporary blindness to the truth.

Later that same day, I found myself alone in the tackroom with Mo Mogaran. She attacked the subject of Dance with a bluntness I did not like.

"Sell Dance, Lucy. He's going to prove too much for you to handle."

"I will not," I retorted. "You were watching us earlier. He went really well."

Mo sighed with exasperation. "There's a big difference between cantering him round a paddock and racing him in a point-to-point."

"We've got weeks to prepare for The Challenge Cup," I commented drily.

"Weeks," repeated Mo sarcastically. "Honey, you need years!"

"You're jealous," I snapped impulsively. Her sarcasm had needled me. "*You* fell off but I can handle him."

I sat back nervously and waited for the explosion of anger but it didn't come. Mo shook her head and half-laughed. "Janey's drivel about you winning the Challenge Cup has really gone to your head, Lucy. But she's the one I blame, not you."

I stared sullenly at the cold cinders in the fire grate. Inwardly, I was wrestling between my honest liking and admiration for Mo and this newly found glamour and reverence that the Challenge Cup had indirectly given me. I knew Mo wasn't jealous. I couldn't con myself into thinking that she was. "I didn't mean what I said, Mo."

She nodded. "That's all right but, Lucy, won't you consider selling him?"

I shook my head. "No, I love him."

We were silent. I was sorry we couldn't agree but I was also determined to stand my ground.

"I'm not going to be around during the next few weeks," she explained as she walked across to the small desk by the window. "You know, Lucy, I guessed you'd be this fired up about Dance and the cup, so I got in touch with a friend of mine. She's called Ros and she's about the best there is when it comes to training horses. I've told her all about you and Dance, and she's agreed to meet you – if you want to. She could be a great help. Only I think we'd better keep this as our secret, because Janey wouldn't approve."

"Doesn't she like Ros?" I asked innocently.

"No, she doesn't," said Mo thoughtfully. "So will you promise to keep it as our secret?"

"Yes, I promise."

Mo took out a pen and wrote something on a piece of paper. I watched and waited with excitement and anticipation. She pushed the paper into my hand and said mysteriously, "I feel as if I owe you this much.

It is partly my fault that you're in this mess with Janey, but take care over these next few weeks. I don't want to land you in any more trouble. Meet Ros but don't tell anyone about it, not even Jo."

She left the tackroom and I opened the folded paper carefully. It read: "Ros Shephard at Manor's Hall Riding School. Two o'clock. Wednesday afternoon."

Chapter Seven
Into the Camp of the Enemy

Dance caused me some trouble that next morning but at least his awful behaviour led me to do some serious thinking. It was a windy day and he was madder than usual. He wanted to gallop and race the wind while I wanted to walk and hide from it. We spun around the tracks like dancing partners. I couldn't do a thing with him. It was the first time I'd taken him out without having someone else with me and it was – as Mo had predicted – a disaster. I eventually dismounted and led him as far as the Long Meadow's lane. Once there I furtively remounted him. I rode into the riding school as if nothing had happened. I didn't want Janey to go hysterical or to see Kay smirk. I suppose I didn't want to come down from my high standing. Later, I did tentatively skirt round the subject with Janey but she wasn't interested. All she cared about were her big plans for me. She wouldn't listen to reason. I could stall her for a short while but not forever. Sooner or later I would have to confront her with my own nagging doubts, which was how I came to re-open the piece of paper Mo had handed to me. It had written on it the name of our worst enemies, Manor's Hall. My initial response then was harsh and dismissive but now I began to truly wonder. I had to accept two things, Janey was unreasonable in the extreme and Dance was a good horse who I believed in but couldn't manage. It was my love of Dance that tipped the scale and made up my mind to go and meet Ros Shephard. If I wanted to keep him, I had to be able to ride him.

It certainly wasn't that my opinions of Angelica Kent ran any higher than anyone else's at Long Meadows. Janey had told us all we needed to know about her. She was successful but, according to Janey, her success had come at a high price. She was ruthless in competition and when she wanted a result badly enough she'd follow any path on earth to get it. We hated her. We hated the snobby little kids that went to her model riding school. The idea of my sneaking up there with Dance, left me in a cold sweat. I was sure that even in Jo's eyes it would brand me as a traitor.

By the Wednesday lunchtime I was trying very hard to justify what I was still intending to do. Jo found me in the hay-barn in a pensive mood.

"Hy'a," she murmured as she sprawled in the hay beside me. "What's up with you today? Janey's worried that you're sick. If you dropped down dead, she'd lose her main chance in The Challenge Cup. She thinks that would be very selfish of you."

"I'm not sick. I've been thinking about Angelica Kent . . ."

"That *is* sick," interrupted Jo quickly.

"Why is it? What has she ever really done to us?" I asked.

"She's pinched Janey's customers," replied Jo. "And Janine Rich bashed Dee that time in the village."

"You can't stand Dee!" I laughed. "Anyway, that was nothing to what Kay did to Janine."

"Ok, I'll give you that," said Jo, sitting up. "But Angelica did once try to run Janey down in her Range Rover, and she did call the police and complain that we were trespassing on her rotten land."

"We were trespassing. Janey sent us to disrupt their riding lessons. Pawn bought about 100 balloons and we floated them over their indoor riding school. It could have been dangerous . . ."

Jo burst out laughing. "It's always been like that between Angelica and Janey. They're sworn enemies. Angelica Kent deserves all she gets. She's a horrible woman."

I was silent for a moment and then I said, "But you've never actually met her, Jo."

"No, but I know she is . . ." Jo trailed off and our eyes met. I was suddenly desperate to tell her that I intended to go to Manor's Hall that afternoon but instead I got to my feet.

"I'd better saddle Dance, I'm going out soon."

"I'll come with you," Jo said lightly.

"No, don't," I said, "not today, I'm planning on going a long way . . ."

It was three long miles to Manor's Hall and as I rode my stomach churned. I repeatedly told myself I was being a fool. If I happened to come across the so-called witch Angelica, I'd be as cold as ice. I was going there for Dance's sake, not mine.

I rode on to the dusty, rutted farm track which led through the aptly named Hope End Farm. This was where the Challenge Cup race was to take place. There were already a few low fly fences erected and as I pulled Dance up to gaze at them, I easily imagined

55

myself jumping them with the roar of the crowd behind me. I stroked Dance's neck. He'd gone remarkably quietly so far and once again my old arrogance resurfaced and I wondered if I had any real need for Mo Mogaren or her friend, Ros Shephard. I rode off the farm and onto the narrow hilly lane which wound past Manor's Hall House. This dangerously thin road was bordered on both sides by tall stone walls and it was because of Dance's height that I could see over the top. There was a professionally coloured show jumping course in the field. It caught my wild imagination as quickly as the racing jumps had. In the near distance on the brow of the hill there was an enormous white house which towered majestically over the valley. This was where Angelica Kent and her husband lived. I knew from our various clandestine attacks on the place, that there were two main entrances, one led to the house and the other which was lower down, to the riding school. There was also a grassy bridleway which ran adjacent to the house. I decided to keep as low a profile as possible and go in by that entrance. Dance was growing increasingly interested. He could smell and sense the other horses. He clenched his muscles and pricked his ears. His stride grew more sprightly, making me tighten my moist grip on the reins. "Steady now, Dance, steady," I repeated to him. But we still burst epileptically onto the yard of Manor's Hall. Everyone instantly stopped what they were doing to stare at us. Dance was spinning like a top as if he was trying to take in every sight of his new surroundings all in one second! I was nervous and reined him back far too sharply. He backstepped into a door, kicked out and as his hoove whacked the wood leapt into the air. Swarms of

Manor's Hall kids were flocking into the yard to see this entertaining and amusing spectacle. I wished I hadn't come. I was in the camp of the enemy, and suddenly I missed the gang very much. Then the office door opened and out stepped a grey haired woman whom I recognised as Angelica Kent. She frowned at the sight of us but then Dance half-reared and she came forward and took hold of his bridle. There was some sniggering and some snide commentary. The Manor's Hall kids had recognised me and they were loving this free exhibition I was putting on. I grew red and hot and all set for a fight with any one of them.

"You're Lucy Walters?" asked Angelica.

I nodded.

"I'll take you up to the little paddock. Ros is going to be a few minutes late."

As she led the way out of the yard, I couldn't help but pull a face at Janine Rich. She was so conceited and full of herself that she made Kay appear positively modest and shy! She glared back at me and I heard one of her sardonic crowd say, "That horse is far too big for her."

Without a word, Angelica led us through the orchard to a long thin field, just below her gardens and house. It didn't look as if it was normally used for riding. At one end of it there was an outdoor swimming pool and beyond that two hard tennis courts.

As she unlocked the gate it struck me that this was the nearest I'd ever been to her. She'd chased us off her land a few times but then I was a fast runner whom she hadn't a hope of catching. She was much older than Janey but she was fitter and healthier. I could see that much in her sun-tanned face and by the way she moved. I'd purposefully been listening out for other people's opinions on Angelica, I'd even gone as far as asking one or two solicitous questions of my own. I concluded that no-one I'd spoken to must have known her as well as Janey did because all they could tell me about her was strikingly favourable. Everyone knew the kernel of her story. In her hey-day she'd been a top professional show jumper. It was clear that her hey-day was well over now but even through my prejudice I could spot her expertise and professionalism. It attracted me. It was, after all, something I wasn't very used to!

"Have you come by road?" she asked suddenly.

I said I had and she almost tutted.

"He's a very beautiful horse, dear," she commented. "But I can imagine he's a handful. Is he quite safe in traffic?"

I said he was, but she didn't look wholly convinced. When we got into the paddock, she watched us with an expert eye. To my surprise it wasn't overtly critical. It was keen – almost admiring. She ran an expert hand down Dance's leg, which he didn't like very much. He made a disgusted face at her which just made her laugh at him. Her reaction rather surprised me and my planned 'cold as ice' approach melted a little. Dance didn't like the way she was walking around him. He kept bending his neck to follow her progress, when she came round to the front of him again, he made a savage attempt to bite her. I had begun to form a new theory about Dance. Namely that he didn't mind harmless idiots like me but he had a definite aversion for anyone with a hint of professionalism. Angelica had more than a hint and Dance didn't like it! She asked me to trot him up and down which I did. Dance was getting into a very silly mood. He lifted his knees almost up to his chin as he pranced across the meadow.

"He'd make a super eventer," Angelica shouted enthusiastically, as I rode back to her, then she added, "He's full of character, isn't he?"

I was glad she'd remarked on Dance's character. No-one else ever had, but I'd often noticed his quirky nature. He knew exactly who he liked and who he didn't like. It was a firmly drawn line in Dance's head. I'd been lucky enough to fall on the right side of it but it was beginning to dawn on me that this might have less to do with my riding ability than I'd initially supposed.

It was perhaps unfortunate that Angelica's shrewd perception of Dance's character didn't put her off from asking me if she could ride him. I dismounted uneasily. I didn't like the way Dance was eyeing her. When she warned him to behave, he gave her the most withering glare I'd ever seen. I was unable to say anything by way of warning. Angelica was a far better rider than I was, and I wouldn't have dared to even try and tell her about Dance's strange little ways. I could only stand back and watch anxiously.

She'd barely been in the saddle a minute when Dance exploded into his rodeo horse act. It was the same one he'd played out every morning with Mo Mogaran and it had very nearly unseated her. He'd stopped doing it with me. I think he knew I was no match for him at all, but believe me, he threw himself wholeheartedly into it with Angelica Kent. Suddenly in Dance's fierce imagination the innocent swifts and swallows became kamikazi pilots to be avoided at all costs. He charged at the hedge for an escape only to find it had grown a hundred heads. His hooves barely touched the grass as he thrust himself around. Angelica Kent was not a young woman but she clung on as if she was. She hadn't been prepared for this onslaught. It was with steely determination that she collected herself enough to lift one arm and give Dance a sharp whack with her crop. I knew it was a mistake. Dance over-reacted, and at once plotted his revenge. His great thoroughbred legs began to work like pistons as he thundered down the meadow towards the open swimming pool. My hand involuntarily came up over my mouth as I helplessly watched their progress.

Chapter Eight
Kay's News

Dance's intentions were clear to me. He was going to pitch Angelica Kent into her own swimming pool. If he succeeded I would never dare look at her again. I would be barred from every pony event in the county probably for the rest of my life. It was only when Dance was perilously close to the edge of the pool that he swerved. Any lesser rider would have carried on without him. Angelica swerved with him. I prayed he would be satisfied and would bring her back, but he didn't. Instead he careered around the rim of the tennis courts, then at last he came back along the length of the paddock. When he was parallel to me, he stopped as if a ghost had suddenly materialized out of thin air. Angelica slid over his shoulder and slapped the ground. Dance sauntered calmly off and began to eat the heads off dandelions, while I reeled with horror by the fence. My first instinct was to run for it, but I couldn't. I had to walk towards her, face her, apologize for my brute of a horse and only then could I run. With each step closer, my legs became weaker with sheer reluctance. This was the end of Manor's Hall for me. This was probably the end of me!

Angelica was still sitting where Dance had deposited her. She didn't look nearly as dignified as when we'd first met. Her hat was slanted over her nose. Her scarf was twisted under one ear and she was breathing very audibly. I helped her up. Neither of us spoke but she did lean heavily against me. Dance was nearby, chewing hard and gazing at us with mild interest and obvious amusement. I got Angelica to the stile, where she sat and stared disbelievingly at the innocent looking animal who was cropping grass in her own paddock. I searched hopelessly for something adequate to say, eventually I muttered, "I'd better go home."

"You haven't seen Ros yet," replied Angelica, "Don't be silly." Then she nodded towards Dance and said, "Is he always like that?"

"He is a bit wild," I said uncomfortably. "I think he's got too much imagination." My explanation for Dance's behaviour certainly wasn't in the strictly equestrian terms she was used to, but to my surprise she laughed.

"Well, my days of riding old rogues like him are long gone."

"I'm very sorry," I said, genuinely.

"It was entirely my fault." She waved her hand dismissively. "I should have known better. Now please don't tell my niece, Ros. She's been telling me to take things easy. She'll be furious if she hears I've been making a fool of myself. I'm too old for that sort of ride!"

I promised her I wouldn't tell. I was confused. Angelica Kent was simply not matching up with the nasty image I'd always had of her.

I found myself liking her. When I'd caught Dance, we chatted easily together until Angelica said seriously, "If I'd been ten years younger and you'd been ten years older, we could have really made something of this horse, but as it is, Lucy, I think you're too young for him. Wouldn't a smaller pony suit you better?"

I put the reins over his head. "Dance needs me," I said. Angelica smiled thoughtfully but before she could reply a woman shouted to us from the lawn. She came running lightly down the steps towards us. She was the kind of person I had vague hopes of being like when I was older. She was tall, slim and very good looking. She was dressed in casual clothes but they still conspired to make her look more stylish and smart than most people do after spending hours dolling themselves up! Angelica introduced us. She was Ros Shephard, the woman I'd come to meet. I liked her straight off, not just because of the way she looked, but because she warmly admired Dance. Angelica warned her that he was an "old rogue", but she winked at me as she said it.

When Angelica left us, I mounted Dance and was immediately told I was riding with the stirrup leathers too short. It heralded the start of a hard hour's riding. According to Ros, I was doing almost everything wrongly. This came as a harsh blow. I'd heard Mo's opinions of how much of a novice she thought I was, but I'd vainly hoped that Ros wouldn't confirm them.

"Hands, Lucy," she yelled repeatedly, until little beads of perspiration began to trickle down my face. I couldn't help silently questioning whether all this schooling stuff would ever help me win The Challenge Cup. We never rode without stirrups at Long Meadows – it was unheard of. Ros was mercilessly keen on it. I felt she was slowly killing me. Dance's trotting stride was about as springy as a trampoline. I hung on, bouncing like a sack of potatoes. I slipped down one side of the saddle and then bounced all the way round to the other side. When Ros called, "stop", I was about two seconds away from ending up on the ground.

"Have you not ridden without stirrups before?" she asked.

I shook my head, but I suppose I must have still been clinging to a last vestige of belief in my own stirring abilities because I added. "It's impossible! I bet there's no-one on earth who could do it on Dance."

It was a typically rash statement. I was to quickly learn not to throw down such unsubstantiated comments, especially to Ros, but at that time I was still far too much the product of Janey Squires' blindness and my own fierce imagination.

Ros's dark eyes flickered with interest and amusement.

"Jump off him then, and I'll show you."

I instantly regretted my words. I didn't think much of Ros's teaching methods, but I did like her. I didn't want her to end up like Mo Mogaran and Angelica Kent had when they'd ridden Dance. Ros noticed my hesitation, and misunderstanding it said with mild sarcasm, "I'll be careful with him, I promise."

I jumped off and watched Dance prickle with interest as she approached him. I could almost hear him thinking. "Oh good, another expert".

Ros quickly altered the stirrups and mounted. I waited for the eruption. It began at once. He acted like a Russian gymnast. It wouldn't have surprised me if he'd tried a backward flip, he tried everything else. But there was a difference this time and I hadn't made allowance for it. Ros was a great deal younger than Angelica and I have to admit it, she was a much better rider even than Mo. Dance was losing this battle and it didn't take him very long to realize it. When he did he settled into the nicest collected canter I'd ever seen him do. Ros rode him in a hard and concentrated manner, making him do things I hadn't thought he was capable of. When she was satisfied with him, she took away the stirrups and performed the same routine again equally as perfectly. I sighed as I watched them. Both Dance and I had been put in our place. I suddenly accepted how much I had to learn as a rider.

I rode home that evening thoroughly impressed with Manor's Hall and Ros. I'd arranged to meet her again the following afternoon, so I was in an optimistic mood until I rode through the gates of Long Meadows. Janey Squires was sitting on the mounting block, jangling her keys impatiently. I shot a glance at my watch. It was six o'clock. She always locked up at five. I could have kicked myself.

"Had a nice ride?" she asked sarcastically.

"Sorry I'm late," I said. "I forgot the time."

"I wish I could forget the time," she whined. "But don't mind me, after all I've nothing better to do than wait for you!"

"It won't happen again," I muttered.

"Where've you been until this hour?"

"Nowhere," I grunted.

"All afternoon at nowhere," she stared suspiciously, making me feel hot and guilty. In desperation I added, "I galloped him, Janey, and he went like the wind. He's a dead cert for the Challenge Cup."

She softened at once. "I know a good horse when I see one."

I took Dance into the dark stables. Janey sat at her

desk at the other end while I saw to him. I was mad at myself for being this late. It had never been more important for me to be careful, and already I'd blundered. If she so much as dreamt I'd been to Manor's Hall, there'd be scenes that would make all Janey's other tantrums appear mild by comparison.

When I'd fed Dance, I found Janey sitting at her desk staring morosely into space. Being alone with her made me uneasy, but to my surprise she smiled weakly.

"Sorry if I was a little touchy. I'm afraid it's my failing health to blame, and, of course, the heavy burden of running this place."

We walked down the empty lane together and Janey, who was always acrobatic in her mood changes, asked me how I was enjoying riding Dance. She made a staunch attempt at being pleasant which did nothing to lessen my feelings of betrayal and guilt. When we said goodnight she squeezed my arm fondly. "I'm pinning my last hopes on you, Lucy. I hope it's not too much for you to cope with."

I told her it wasn't and we went our separate ways. While I sat on the kerb and waited for the bus I began to speculate about Janey and Angelica's rivalry. I wished I knew more about Janey's reasons for hating Angelica. I was finding it difficult to connect Angelica Kent with all the tales Janey had told us. I still believed, as the gang did, that right had to be on Janey's side. How else could she have come to hate someone as violently as she hated Angelica? What had gone on between the two women was a mystery to me, and yet at that time both riding schools had something I really needed. My friends and my deepest loyalties were with Long Meadows, but Ros and

Dance's only chance was with Manor's Hall. I fully intended to return to Manors' Hall as often as Ros would agree to teach me. It wasn't that I didn't acknowledge the risk involved. It was more that I was mad keen to learn, and hopeful enough to still believe I might have a chance of bringing the Challenge Cup home to Long Meadows and to Janey.

I was up early the next morning and was at Jo's house by seven. She was having breakfast on her own, so I joined her and she told me that Kay Davenport had been up to her old tricks again. Apparently Kay was saying that I would never jump Dance and that the race I'd won against her was a fluke.

"She's such a fool," I exclaimed excitedly. "She doesn't know what she's talking about. Even Ros says I'm not good enough to jump him yet."

"Who's Ros?" asked Jo.

I could have bitten off my tongue. I couldn't believe anyone could prove less effective at keeping secrets than I was.

"She's no-one special."

"She must be someone."

"Everyone's someone," I snapped.

"Um," hummed Jo as if she wasn't sure that they were. "So who is she, Luce, and what does she know about you and Dance?"

"She's no-one," I moaned. "And she knows nothing."

"If everyone's someone, she can't be no-one," mocked Jo just before I threw a piece of toast at her. It had the desired effect of changing the subject. I hoped that it wouldn't crop up again, only it did, and this time at a far more critical moment. We'd all just had lunch and Janey came into the tackroom clutching her unpopular, slave labour, grass picking rota. Somehow the conversation veered from picking grass to jumping Dance. It wasn't Kay's doing this time, she'd gone to the village shop. Janey was telling me how I would have to get in some serious practice before the Big Day when Jo in all innocence said, "Luce has a mysterious new friend called Ros who says she isn't ready to jump Dance."

Janey fixed me with a stare that might have stopped an approaching army. "Who is Ros?" she asked quietly.

My mouth opened. I was all ready to spin any one of the mad fictional stories that were racing across my mind when the tackroom door was almost torn from its hinges. We all jumped in surprise and Janey's taut nerves looked fit to snap.

"What the . . ." she began.

Kay was standing in the doorway, flushed pink and rather breathless. She interrupted Janey's storm of protest by shouting, "Janey, I've just been talking to Janine Rich and she's told me a devastating piece of news."

The cup I was holding slipped out of my hands. It hit the floor and crashed into a jigsaw puzzle of jagged pieces. The news had to be about me. What else would Janine Rich from Manor's Hall have to tell Kay Davenport? There was no way out of the room, so I ducked my head and with trembling hands began picking up the broken china.

"Angelica has bought a racehorse to enter into the Challenge Cup, just so that she can beat you."

I lifted my head in amazement. I knew nothing of this and I found it difficult to believe Angelica would care to that extent about any competition. Again, i didn't fit with the image of the woman I'd met. She had nothing to prove.

"She's just done this to you, Janey," said Kay emotively. "She can't stand the idea that for once we could steal some of the limelight from her!"

I was mesmerised by Janey. She was pale and gaunt, almost eaten from the inside with her hatred and envy. I could see her so clearly it scared me. Her fury metamorphosised into an attack on Angelica which all but demanded revenge.

"She won't win! She won't win!" Janey cried, and the gang, who were by now all equally heated, took up her chant with a vengeance I'd not witnessed before.

Chapter Nine
Home Truths

I listened quietly as the room rang with pure hatred for Angelica Kent. The gang were suddenly more animated than Janey. They were demanding the revenge she'd been careful only to hint at.

"Burn Manor's Hall to the ground," cried Dee wildly.

"Kidnap her rotten racehorse," shouted Michelle.

The suggestions got madder by the minute until Janey held up her hands, and said, "Girls, we can't break the law. We'll have to think of some other way."

"We could win," suggested Jo sensibly.

"But we must be sure of winning," said Janey. "I can't afford to lose this race." She glanced anxiously at me as if she was sizing up her only chance.

Kay said eagerly, "Lucy can't even jump. At least I can!"

"You can't," I snapped back. "When have you ever jumped Max over anything bigger than a puddle?"

"Oh, anyone can jump," said Janey carelessly. "The horse does all the work. All you have to do is lean forward and hang on."

Jo sniggered at this but I couldn't help comparing Janey's fatuous comment with Angelica's professional and careful approach. There was a world of difference

70

I was beginning to wonder if Janey had any notion of what she was talking about. Even Kay had her doubts.

"Are you sure there isn't more to it than that?" she asked with a frown.

"I did once ride at Hickstead," Janey replied in a lofty way. "Those were my halcyon days, Kay, when I was at my athletic peak."

It was truly hard to imagine Janey at her athletic peak. It made me wonder what had happened since to rollercoast her into this crumbling state of decline.

"Didn't Janine Rich tell you anything else about this racehorse, Kay?" asked Pawn, neatly taking us away from Janey's dewy eyed memories.

"Only that Angelica has bought him for her niece. I can't remember her first name but her last name is Shephard."

"Ros Shephard," said Janey and everyone turned to stare at me.

"What are you all looking at me for?" I asked in as innocent a tone as I could muster.

"You mentioned someone called Ros who has been giving you advice," Dee replied coldly.

"No-one from Manor's Hall," I said indignantly. "I wouldn't be seen dead at Manor's Hall. I hate them. You all know that." I was lying desperately and throwing my whole self into making it sound convincing.

"That's true," said Jo loyally. "She wouldn't touch them with a barge pole, would you, Luce?"

"No," I muttered uncomfortably.

"Who is she, then?" asked Kay sharply.

"She's a friend of my Mum's. She came round to our house last night. She was telling me that she used

71

to own a horse and we got talking about Dance. She didn't think he sounded ready to be jumped."

Janey grunted, and Jo smiled in a relieved way. The subject switched back to The Challenge Cup and I was able to sit back in the chair and be thankful that they had bought my story.

One thing I'd long since learnt about Janey was that there was an awesome gap between what she said she'd do and what she did. As the days passed her incongruous plans to tear Angelica's hair out and to drag the name of Manor's Hall through the mud, festered into a more resigned sore. If Angelica Kent wanted to buy her niece a racehorse, there was nothing anyone could do to stop her, however annoying it might be. It gnawed at Janey's nerve ends though. It meant that The Challenge Cup was not simply ours for the taking. Janey had relied on our racehorse being the only one. Now it seemed he had real competition. Janey took to going off with Kay for secret talks. I was really scared that they were plotting something against Angelica. They made a dangerous and cunning partnership. They wanted to see Dance galloped. They wanted to see him jumped. They wanted constant reassurances that I would be able to manage him in time for The Challenge Cup. I was able to satisfy their expectations, at least in part, thanks to Ros's help. Under her guidance Dance was improving tremendously but I still hadn't jumped him. Everyone at Long Meadows, including Jo, were so blinkered by Janey's view that they didn't think it mattered that no-one had actually taught me *how* to jump. It was ironic that Manor's Hall were the enemy and yet it was the only place where I found anything like solace. By the end of that week all of us at Long Meadows were under strain. The weather had begun to change and the forecast was bad. It made Janey worse. She was worried about one part of the stable roof. It was at the point of collapse and any really heavy weather would finish it off. Riding lessons had dwindled to an all time low and we couldn't even pick grass to help supplement the feed. It was against this backcloth that each day I escaped to Manor's Hall and my new, valued friend – Ros.

One such afternoon, when the rain was drizzling and my concentration wasn't proving inspirational, Ros suggested we put Dance into a loose box while we went and had a cup of tea. I can't say I was sorry to do this. My riding seemed to embrace every bad habit known to man. I was a textbook example of how not to ride! I told myself the problem was I had too much on my mind.

I increasingly felt that I was being split in two between Long Meadows and Manor's Hall. Janey's worries about the stable roof had infected me, but more I felt that the gang were growing suspicious about my long, regular afternoon rides. I'd even heard some of their whispered rumours and, believe me, they were getting near to the mark. Also, it was becoming harder for me to conceal my guilty feeling that I was betraying their friendship, even though I was only here for the purpose of learning to ride Dance as well as I possibly could before The Challenge Cup. Ros chatted on unconscious of my confusion.

"You and Dance are doing really well, Luce," she said kindly.

"I'm a shambles," I said.

Ros laughed. "You need some more practice, that's all. Give it time."

73

"But that's what I haven't got," I exclaimed. "The Challenge Cup is only two weeks away."

Ros slid a cup of tea across the large kitchen table towards me and said, "What's that got to do with anything?"

I paused. Since first meeting Ros I'd had a feeling she didn't know anything about my plans to enter for The Challenge Cup. If Mo Mogaran had failed to tell her, I didn't think I ought to be the one to break the startling news. At the same time, I drew a hard and fast line at telling her lies. Fortunately Angelica's cat came to my rescue by crying to be let out. Ros had to go and open both of the outer doors. It was a perfectly timed distraction. When she returned I was able to steer the conversation onto slightly more neutral ground.

"Do you think Dance would have a chance in The Challenge Cup?" I asked innocently.

Ros sipped her tea before answering. "I think he would," she said before adding, "But don't *you* get any mad ideas about entering it. The very thought would give me sleepless nights!"

"Am I that hopeless?" I said, stung with indignation.

"No, but you haven't the experience for something like a point to point race. The jumps are small enough in The Challenge Cup, but it's still a very competitive race and I have a feeling that this time it's going to be a free for all. I don't fully approve of this year's prize money. It's been donated by an anonymous local business man but fifteen hundred pounds as a first prize is bound to turn what has always been a fun race into a deadly serious competition!"

I stared at Ros. "F . . . f . . . fifteen hundred

pounds?" I stuttered, and suddenly I understood why Janey was so keen for me to win.

"It's far too much," smiled Ros unsuspectingly.

"It'll all go to the riding school that the winning rider represents, but normally the prize money only totals about fifty pounds."

I drank my tea as if in a dream. I wondered if Janey had concealed the amount of prize money from me purposely. We were silent as I digested the information and thought not for the first time about Janey's motives.

"Long Meadows are entering," I told her with a small revival of pride. "Janey really needs the money."

The expression on Ros's face changed the moment I mentioned Janey's name. Her lip curled with distaste. It was partly her reaction and partly a result of my own muddled loyalties that I felt needled enough to say, "It's not Janey's fault she can't compete with this place. Janey isn't rich like Angelica is!"

"Isn't that rather an assumption on your part?"

"It's true enough," I shrugged. "Janey was doing really well until Angelica started to put her out of business."

Ros's dark eyes flickered emotively as they bore into mine, then she said quietly, "It strikes me you don't know the whole story. But take my word for it, this mess Janey's in has nothing whatsoever to do with Angelica."

"How can you say that?" I exclaimed angrily. "It's a lie!" I was surprised by my own bubbling emotions, but they were on behalf of the underdog, Janey.

"Angelica's gone out of her way to help Janey," retorted Ros sharply. "The reason why she's never taken liveries is to give Janey a chance to build up that side of her business free from any competition!"

"B . . . but if that's right," I almost stuttered, "why does Janey hate Angelica so much?"

Ros sighed. "It's a long story," she said dismissively.

"Tell it to me, Ros," I said. "Please, it's very important that I know."

Ros got up and walked to the Aga where she poured more water into the teapot. I fidgeted impatiently with the ring on my finger until she came and sat down.

"Well, six years ago both Janey and Angelica applied to the same bank for separate loans. Angelica wanted to set up Manor's Hall and Janey wanted to expand Long Meadows. Neither of them knew anything at all about the other's plans."

"But Janey didn't get her loan, did she?" I said.

"No. The bank turned down Janey's application and they accepted Angelica's. When Janey got to hear of this she blamed Angelica's so-called power and influence for turning the bank against her. She broadcast her bitterness and envy throughout the county. Angie was naturally upset by these accusations, so much so that she went to see the Bank Manager. He told her, albeit off-the-cuff, that Janey's loan had been turned down for quite separate reasons. He happened to believe there *was* enough business in the county for both riding schools."

"Doesn't Janey know the truth?" I asked.

"Oh, she knows," replied Ros. "It suits her to go on blaming Angie for her own failures. I'm afraid, Lucy, that I'm not nearly as generous as my aunt is, when it comes to Janey Squires. I know how much trouble the darned woman has caused."

I certainly could never blame Ros for not thinking charitably about Janey or Long Meadows. We'd done everything we could to make life tougher for poor Angelica. If it hadn't been for Mo's tenuously surviving friendship with Ros there would have been no bridge at all between the two stables and I'd have never found out the truth. It shocked me. I'd really fought against liking Manor's Hall and all because of hearsay. It was as if I'd been under a long spell cast by a witch. Now that it was broken I was bound to share my findings.

When I got back to Long Meadows, I dragged Jo into a quiet corner. But before I'd even begun she broached the same subject with some startling news.

"Janey's got it into her head that this Ros you mentioned is Angelica Kent's niece and that you've been sneaking off to see her," she whispered urgently. "Kay's egging her on like mad, but I told her it's rubbish."

"It's true, Jo," I said excitedly.

"What?"

"I've been going to Manor's Hall every afternoon to meet Ros."

"Don't fool on, Luce. This is serious."

"I'm not. I mean it."

"I don't believe it. You wouldn't," said Jo, and she pulled back from me.

"Why wouldn't I?"

"Because, you fool, they're our worst enemies!"

"They're not, Jo. Everything Janey's told us is total drivel. Angelica's really great. She's even tried to help Janey by never taking liveries. The whole rotten feud was caused because Janey couldn't accept the truth!" I met Jo's eyes hopefully.

"You sucker," she exploded. "Of course they're going to tell you it isn't their fault. Did you really expect them to say it was?"

I didn't answer and Jo swung abruptly away from me and began to walk off. I went after her and caught hold of her arm.

"Jo, you're not going to tell Janey or any of the others, are you?"

"I won't tell," she murmured, but she still shook me loose with a coldness that hurt me more than any words could.

Chapter Ten
The Witch's Brew

That night the heavens opened, and as Janey had predicted, part of the roof at Long Meadows came crashing down. Nor did the catastrophic rain ease. It came out of the sky as if bent solely on destroying the last remnants of Janey's struggle.

At first she was all hiss and flick knife nails like a tormented ginger cat. She darted from under one part of the leaking roof to another with her hair dripping its red dye down her neck. As the rain continued and the sodden morning wore on, Janey's determination began to see-saw wildly into despair. She huddled in front of the no-smoking sign, her tough, trembling fingers clutching a cigarette in one hand and a cup of coffee in the other.

"I think the worst's over," shouted Pawn optimistically.

"We'll clean up for you, Janey," said Arab keenly.

"It'll be alright," promised Kay, "we'll have the place as good as new in no time."

"Can you mend roofs?" Janey retorted sullenly.

Janey went home eventually to try and find the address of a very cheap roofer. She left us to battle not only against the damage from the storm, but by now against one another. Tempers were short and quick. Jo wasn't speaking to me which was arousing speculative comments and interest, and Kay and Arab were playing a kind of tug of war game over who should be in charge. It was Michelle who suggested a temporary truce. She pointed out that this was an emergency and Janey needed us. I expected Kay to stamp Chelle into one of the numerous puddles that had formed while we fought but it is usually the unexpected that happens.

"Chelle's right," said Kay grandly. "If Long Meadows closes, what will happen to the ponies?"

So we formed our truce and for a short while we worked together like the ace team we once were. I hadn't thought it possible that I'd feel the return of any loyalty towards Janey or Long Meadows but I did. I was surprised by how much I enjoyed that hard morning. We ran in and out with buckets and continued digging a channel for the water to run into the drains from. Then at about one o'clock, the rain eased, and shortly after that the pale sun came out. We were about as celebratory as if we'd won a first prize. We danced around, yelling happily. The worst was over and I don't think I'd ever felt closer to the gang. It was very short lived. When Janey returned she was as sour as old milk. She'd found a roofer but he wasn't going to be as cheap as she'd hoped. It would be another bill to add to the huge list, another debt in the making. She barely noticed our efforts on her behalf. When she saw me struggling with a full bucket of water, she turned angrily on Kay.

"Take that heavy bucket from little Lucy. She might strain herself and then what would happen to The Challenge Cup?"

I could have died there and then with embarrassment. Kay was understandably mad. "What about me? I'm riding in it too or had you forgotten?"

"Let's face it Kay. *You* haven't got any real chance of winning, have you?" Janey muttered.

Both Kay and I were rendered temporarily speechless by Janey's directness. I hoped Kay might take it out on Janey but when she turned to face me I knew that wasn't her style.

"Let me take that," she sneered. "We don't want you to sprain your little wrist. Buckets are such dangerous things in the wrong hands."

"Get off," I said quietly. "I can carry it easily."

"No you can't," Kay tutted making the others laugh.

"No you mustn't," piped up Janey.

Our two grips on the bucket's handle became competitive. Kay pulled one way and I pulled the other. Only she let go at the crucial moment, and the whole lot tipped over me. Everyone burst out laughing except Janey. She pointed at my soaking wet jeans and exclaimed in a shrill voice, "She's all wet." This made everyone laugh all the louder.

"She'll catch her death," Janey hollered. "Then where will we be?"

Her concern for me was so touching it made me want to throw the bucket at her. It didn't stop there either. She was actually genuinely annoyed – with me!

"What's the matter with you, child?" she bawled. "Why didn't you let Kay help you? She was only trying to be kind."

"She was not!" I yelled back.

"I was, Lucy," smiled Kay. "I wish you'd trust me a little more."

"It looked to me, Kay," said Jo suddenly, "as

81

though you almost threw that bucket over Lucy." She was leaning in a 'couldn't care less' stance by the stable door and I'd barely noticed her. Now our eyes met and I smiled gratefully. Kay glared huffily at her, and Janey grunted in disapproval, but the row fizzled out. I went to the tackroom to get dry, wondering if Jo's intervention signalled the end to our fight. Later though, she came in and treated me with the same coldness as before. I was disappointed.

"Thanks for sticking up for me," I said tentatively.

"It was just the truth," Jo shrugged. "It's no big deal."

"Oh c'mon, Jo," I cried out, impatiently. "This is no fun. Janey's off her head. Kay's got it in for me. I'm sunk without you on my side."

"Aren't Manor's Hall enough?"

"Why don't you give them a chance? Come with me tomorrow."

"And get caught up with the likes of Janine Rich and Elspeth Montgomery. Not likely! That's where you belong, Luce, now you've got Dance, but I could never belong with that bunch. They're snobs!"

"Thanks," I said drily. "So you're saying I belong with a bunch of snobs."

"It seems that way."

"I had to learn how to ride, didn't I? There was precious little help here. You all expected me to go out and win The Challenge Cup for you, to hell with the fact that I couldn't even manage Dance."

"Who are you going to win it for, Angelica or Janey?" growled Jo sarcastically.

"I'm going to win it for *me*, Jo! Not for Janey, not for Angelica and not for you and the gang, but for Dance and for me. I'm sick to death of hearing people tell me that Dance is too wild and I'm too much of a novice to stand a chance. I'm fed up with the whole lot of you!" I didn't wait to hear Jo's reply. I stormed out as close to tears as I've ever been in her company.

I thought we were probably finished as friends, and it was yet another thing to blame on Janey Squires. I did blame her very bitterly. Only I underestimated Jo because about an hour later she came to find me. I wasn't looking forward to any more trouble with her so I was defensive and the atmosphere was strained, with deep feelings on both sides. Jo was obviously uncomfortable about whatever she wanted to say to me. I was uncomfortable about hearing it, but I needn't have been.

"I'm sorry," she said at last, as she pushed her hand through her dark spikey hair.

"Forget it," I said quite enthusiastically.

"Well, I've been thinking . . ."

"Did it hurt?" I interrupted cheerfully.

Jo ignored me. "I've been thinking about what you said and you're right. I suppose I can understand why you needed Manor's Hall. I think I will come with you tomorrow."

Jo's change of heart made all the difference to me. I was certain that once she met Angelica and Ros she would come to alter her views just like I had. Jo was staying that night at her Aunt Cleo's house and so we arranged to meet at the bus station in town. I was there spot on time but there was no sign of her and eventually I had to get the bus on my own. I wasn't too worried. I thought she'd probably slept in again and that she would catch up with me at Long Meadows. But she never did. When I set off for Manor's Hall I was feeling very let down. I knew Jo didn't like Janine Rich and I couldn't help wondering if she'd changed her mind and decided not to bother with them or me.

Manor's Hall seemed a hive of excitement and activity. Ros and Janine were in the yard with the most beautiful and mettlesome black horse I've ever seen. Ros explained to me he was a gift to her from Angelica. His name was Jet.

"Is this the racehorse you're entering into The Challenge Cup?" I asked, and Ros said he was.

I was impressed. He was about an inch smaller than Dance but he was much younger. There wasn't a scrap of fat on him. He was all lithe muscle and his legs were fine and hard. As I admired him, Ros told me Janine Rich would be riding him in The Challenge Cup. Janine stood nearby looking very smug and self satisfied. I think in many people's books she was the firm favourite to win. She was undeniably a very good rider but never particularly modest about it. Ros saddled Jet and asked if I minded going out for a hack instead of schooling Dance. I didn't mind in the least. It was a dry, hot August morning and both the horses were fresh and fit. I watched Jet with interest. Perhaps he was Dance's main competition. I felt alternatively sneaky to be sizing him up and deeply curious to know how fast he was. We rode through the shady cool pine woods until it brought us into an enormous field, hazy with morning heat. It had a track along one side of it where the tractors came and went.

"Is Jet fast?" I asked.

Ros assured me he was. The horses were side by side and tensing like coiled springs because they wanted to gallop.

"I bet he's not as fast as Dance," I said with a grin. "Dance has never lost a race in his life."

"You're getting very cocky, Luce," laughed Ros.

We had reached the first corner. There was the slightest breath of breeze which tantalized the horses. We were turning into the longest length of the field. It stretched ahead of us like a racecourse made for two. My reins were taut as Dance strained against them. We broke into a canter and Ros shouted "Take it steadily."

Even if I'd wanted to I couldn't have. Dance's stride grew and grew until we were galloping flat out. I leant into his neck as much as I could and I even urged him faster, but we couldn't seem to shake Jet off. He matched us with a burst of speed I hadn't credited him with. As we ate up the long field Jet began to inch very gradually into the lead. Dance gave his all to bring us level with him, but again Jet gained ground. We galloped into the last corner clearly behind Jet, and then Ros began to pull him up and I did the same with Dance.

"Well ridden, Luce," Ros shouted when we'd come to a halt.

"I lost," I said, like someone in a dream.

"Don't take it so seriously. Dance went beautifully and you managed to stop him perfectly well. You ought to be proud."

"But I lost," I muttered again.

Fortunately Ros was patting Jet and she didn't appear to hear. As we rode home all I could think, was that The Challenge Cup was not going to be mine after all. It was going to go to Manor's Hall just as it always had.

Chapter Eleven
The Great Escape

I left Manor's Hall that afternoon with my childish pride in tatters but much worse was to come. I was deep in thought about how I'd lost to Jet when someone leapt out of the undergrowth, startling both me and Dance. He shied so sharply that I fell off. I felt a bit foolish, sitting there in the dust, clinging to his reins. I was all ready to blast the idiot who'd scared him, only when I looked up it was to be met by Kay Davenport. She was quickly joined by Arab. There was no point in denying it now. I was caught red-handed, leaving Manor's Hall by their own private bridleway. I got to my feet slowly, almost reluctantly.

"I've just been visiting a friend," I explained. "There's no harm in that, is there?"

"Janey said we'd find you here," replied Arab. "I didn't believe her. You know how she feels about this place, how we all feel."

"Don't tell her, then. Why upset her?" I asked carelessly as I flung the reins over Dance's head. I took hold of the stirrup as if to mount but Kay swung me back making me stagger. It wasn't exactly a violent action, but it had a heavy hint of threat to it.

"I always knew you'd sell us out," she hissed.

"I have not!" I exploded. "Janey's lied to all of us. Angelica's not the enemy. She never was!"

I was wasting my breath. Neither Kay nor Arab would believe me. It was like trying to convince someone of the truth after they've been brainwashed to believe lies. They shared a knowing glance with one another. Kay shook her head sadly.

"I've had it with you," she said icily. "Ever since you got Dance you've thought you're something so special. After everything Janey's done for you, all you do for her is to swop to her enemy's side. I call that pretty low . . ."

"I haven't swopped sides," I interrupted in exasperation.

"Well, don't think you're on ours any more," Kay retorted sharply. She was having trouble controlling her bitterness towards me.

"I happen to know that Jo's blown you out already," she continued. "When Janey finds out, you'll be finished at Long Meadows. Your new found friend – Angelica Kent doesn't take liveries, so what are you going to do with Dance? You'll be all on your lonely own, won't you?"

She thumped the palm of her hand into my shoulder as if to stamp her enemity on me. As she turned to go something in me snapped. I let Dance's reins fall and I jumped on her. She was much bigger than I was, but I caught her by surprise. We swayed like a couple of wrestlers locked in combat. I kicked her in the shin, but she suddenly thrust me backwards. I charged at her again, swinging my fist into her nose and then quickly darted out of the way of her mad-bull wrath. Arab dived in between us and forcibly restrained Kay who was bright red especially round the nose. After a minute of hectic to-ing and fro-ing on their behalf, Kay poked a warning finger at me. "Don't try that again. Just don't try that again!"

She swung away, truly ruffled and heated, and I went after her. It wasn't courage. Thought had long since given precedence to raw emotion. I leap frogged on to her back and hung round her neck. She wheeled furiously, plucking at me all the time. She meant business too. When she'd dragged me off, she flung herself at me with violent intent. Arab danced around us, yelling "Stop". I didn't stand a chance, within seconds I was knocked dizzily into the grass.

Arab yelled, "She's half your size, Kay. Get off her!"

Kay stopped by the track. Her face was set, her breath came in panting gasps. "I was just defending myself," she exclaimed. "She started it."

"I don't call that defending yourself," retorted Arab. Kay was embarrassed by what had happened. She hadn't seriously hurt me, but she rushed off as if she had. Arab hoisted me to my feet.

"Are you off your head?" she asked. "You know what Kay's like!"

"I'm not scared of her," I mumbled, though it wasn't strictly true.

"Luce, just get Dance and ride back to Long Meadows. I'll try and catch up with Kay before she exaggerates this whole episode to Janey. O.K.?"

I nodded. "Thanks," I called weakly, as she chased off after Kay.

I didn't believe an army could stop Kay from doing exactly as she pleased nor did I relish the idea of riding into the reception Kay would have arranged for me. I desperately needed the advice of a sane, sensible person, which is why I turned towards Manor's Hall and went to look for Ros. She wasn't there. Janine told me Ros and Angelica had driven into town. Apparently they were going to some important dinner dance that evening. I waited for nearly an hour, but when they still didn't come back I accepted my fate and rode to Long Meadows.

It was like riding into a ghost town. The stable doors tapped against their frames as the breeze began to pick up some strength. The hay nets had been dropped even before being filled. A wheelbarrow was left in the middle of the yard and a pitchfork was stabbed ominously into the muck heap. I led Dance through the deserted stables to his loose box, and after I'd seen to him, I trailed to the paddock. I had an ever deepening sense of foreboding. The mere sight of the tackroom gave me an intuitive belief that they were all in there, discussing me. Stealthily, almost furtively, I went towards the closed door and sure enough, their chorus of raised voices quickly reached me. The tackroom had never been such a threatening place to me as it was now. I weakened at the very thought of opening that door. Something in me still wanted to belong to the close knit gang of Long Meadows. I would have much preferred to have been on the inside and safe with them, than lonely on the outside like this. My brain told me not to go any further but my heart, foolish and instinctive as ever, propelled me into throwing open the door. At once the room pitched into silence. Janey was the only person to move. She came towards me. Her eyes were like two little stones with red rims that smarted. They never left my face as she stepped through the crowded muddle to reach me. I held my breath but my heart hammered all the harder for it.

"Lucy, you look worn out. Come on in and have a nice cup of tea."

She directed me towards a chair. Pawn poured the tea at Janey's nod of command. I glanced dartingly at Kay. She was filing her nails, with faked concentration. Suddenly, Jo got up and slammed her way out of the room. Janey ignored her.

"Kay's told us about how you've been going to Manor's Hall. Lucy, I'm a reasonable woman. You needn't have secrets from me." She hesitated, drawing long and hard on her cigarette before fixing me with a reptilian stare. "Do you still intend to represent Long Meadows in our glorious attempt to take The Challenge Cup from Manor's Hall?" She asked it mildly as if she was asking me to pass the sugar but it was the million dollar question.

"Yes," I said. "I tried to explain that to Kay . . ."

"Not another word," interrupted Janey with a beaming smile. "Except to say this. I won't have bad feelings in our happy little team, so I want you and Kay to shake hands and bury the hatchet. Right?"

I was doubtful about Janey. She sounded more like some hale and hearty Brown Owl than the cunning old witch I now knew she was. Still, it was a much needed reprieve. I met Kay's glassy stare. She stood up, so did I. She pushed out her chubby hand, with its rings on every finger, and I took it. She squeezed much too hard, crunching my fingers in her grip. Her smile said "I hate you", and I smiled the same sort of smile back at her. Janey was well satisfied though.

"That's the ticket," she said. "Now let's please put all this nastiness behind us. I always say there's far too much hatred in this world without our adding to it."

We trooped out of the tackroom, at least outwardly

reunited by Janey's attempt at bridge mending. She didn't entirely fool me but I was so relieved that things hadn't been worse that I was willing to accept the uneasy peace. I did wonder why Jo had walked out. When I went to help the others make up the horses' feed I was surprised to find that she was as cold as ice towards me. She pulled away if I brushed against her and made cutting retorts to anything I said. Janey tutted at her but Janey could have tutted for the rest of her days and it wouldn't have stopped Jo.

I fed Dance in a mechanical and blank way and leant on the stable door to watch him eat. I didn't even bother to look towards the sound of light running footsteps so I got quite a shock when someone grabbed my arm. It was Jo and she seemed nervous.

"I thought you weren't speaking to me," I grunted.

"Shh," she hissed. "It was just an act. I thought I'd better keep it up because Janey still doesn't trust me."

"What are you talking about?"

"She's as mad as a hatter, Luce. I had to pretend that we'd fallen out or she wasn't going to let me stay and listen while they discussed you."

I struggled to calm my panic, and said, "But she's been all right with me."

Jo paused uncomfortably. She stroked Dance's shoulder pensively before meeting my eyes. "She tricked us. That first time we saw Dance, he'd been doped. Fred Mannering is one of Mo's more crooked friends. It was done so he'd be nice and docile when we handled him."

"I don't believe it," I protested weakly, but the truth was I did believe her. I just didn't want to.

"Don't you see, Janey wanted you to have a horse that could win her the first prize of £1,500 in The

91

Challenge Cup," continued Jo in a rushed voice. "She never dreamt that there'd be more than one racehorse entered in it!"

"Were the others in on it?" I asked with a tensely indrawn breath.

"Just Janey and Mo Mogaran," replied Jo. "But the gang are in on it now. Janey's as mad as hell about you going up to Manor's Hall. She's going to hold fire until you win her the money and The Challenge Cup, then she plans to kick you out of Long Meadows, that very same night!"

"She can't do that!" I exclaimed but it was a half hearted protest.

"She's barmy, she'd do anything. Anyway would you really want to stay here knowing how she's used you?"

"The gang would stick up for me."

"Oh, c'mon, Luce," said Jo impatiently. "Janey and Kay are quite a double act when they get going. They can wrap the gang around their little fingers. Janey has a real talent of making it sound like she's in the right and the rest of the world's in the wrong!"

I felt bewildered, as if the world had moved ever so slightly on its axis without my realizing it, and that the summer with its once ripening hopes had dissolved while I'd been elsewhere, doing other things. I felt injured, let down and weakened by the gang's betrayal of me. Jo was tougher. "We've got to get out of here tonight," she told me strongly. "Surely Angelica would stable Dance for at least one night?"

I nodded confusedly.

"You get ready to leave. I'll give you the word when everyone's at least out of the stables. You may have to ride hard, Luce, so I'll meet up with you at Manor's Hall."

"She's bound to come after us," I shivered.

"If she does it'll have to be either on foot or horse-back. The van's leaking petrol, so she can't drive it."

"Jo, do you think we're doing the right thing? I'm scared, she'll hit the roof when she realizes what we're up to."

"What else can we do? We can't stay," replied Jo, her eyes sparkling at the thought of the adventure ahead. As she hurried off to act as my look out, I saddled Dance, flung our belongings into a bag and tried to digest all that Jo had told me. I was reminded of Janey's debt to Sam Nailer, of the cryptic conversation I'd overheard her and Mo having, and the switch in Dance's behaviour from when I'd first seen him to when he arrived. There was no doubting Janey's guilt. I wondered if I could ever forgive her. At that moment, standing alone in the darkening stables, I thought not.

"It's all clear," called Jo.

I led Dance out of Long Meadows for what I imagined would be the last time. The clatter of his hooves was undisguisable. I pulled the leathers down with trembling hands. Janey came shooting out of the barn, with a pitchfork still in her hand.

"You can't take Dance out at this hour, Lucy. I'm sorry but this is my riding school and we have to abide by some rules. I forbid it!" I mounted Dance and said with an eruption of feeling, "You can go to hell."

Janey's bottom jaw fell open. "W . . . w . . . what did you say to me, you little madam?"

"We're walking out on you, Janey," explained Jo with a vibrant thrill in her voice. "I've told Luce everything."

Janey instantly dropped the pitchfork and pushed Jo roughly aside. She took hold of my leg and began dragging me out of the saddle. "You're not going anywhere," she yelled.

"Shut that gate," she ordered to the gang who had gathered to see what the fuss was all about.

"You can't keep us here," I panted, and I tried to wrestle her bony grip from my leg. I was very nearly pulled out of the saddle when Jo knocked into Janey, shoving her out of the way.

"Go on, Luce. Ride!" Jo shouted.

Arab and Dee had the five bar gate firmly secured. I searched for another exit. Kay and I both spotted it at the same moment. She began to sprint to block it off while I scrambled Dance up and down the sloping edges of the muck heap. An outraged yell from Jo made me stop Dance and look towards her. She was side stepping Janey's crazy temper and I watched anxiously as she ran to the gate and vaulted over it with an athletic agility our PE teacher would have been proud of. Kay had meanwhile used my hesitation to her advantage. As I turned towards her, I saw with dismay that she'd managed to put a heavy pole across the gap. It was probably about three feet high and she was standing in front of it, gloating. I tightened my grip on the reins and rode Dance at her. She stood stock still, her expression altering as she watched my furious approach. Dance was as fired up as I was and needed little encouragement. Kay left it until the last moment before diving out of the way with a shriek of protest. Dance soared into the air, jumping as if it were Beechers Brook. We landed with a noisy clatter on the tarmac lane and I thanked God no cars had been passing by. Janey's harrowing screams rang in my ears as we flew towards the village but I gave her no heed.

Chapter Twelve
When Sparks Fly

Dance was well lathered by the time I'd reached Manor's Hall. The noise of his hooves on the drive brought Angelica, her husband and Ros all shooting out of the house. They were glamorously dressed in evening clothes, and I suddenly remembered Janine telling me there was an important function on in town that night. In stark comparison I was bruised, dirty and bedraggled. I gave them my 'orphan in the storm' story whilst Dance snorted and even tried to pull a shirt button off Mr Kent. They were very concerned, and Angelica insisted that I stable Dance with them for the time being. She and Ros took me to the stables to show me where everything was kept. We'd just got Dance settled when Mr Kent shouted from the garden that their taxi had arrived. I thanked Angelica for her help, and promised her and Ros that I would wait for Jo and then we'd go home. They seemed anxious about me but Mr Kent was growing impatient and at last they hurried off.

It was seven o'clock. I tried to estimate how long it would take Jo to get to Manor's Hall via Johnson's farm. It was too early to start worrying, but it was the night and the setting for worry. The wind was blowing colder now, studded with September and I was ill at ease in these lonely and largely unfamiliar surroundings. Even Angelica's house began to look strangely forlorn and ominously vacant as I hurried to the far gate to meet Jo. I kept telling myself Janey couldn't come looking for me, but it didn't stop this enveloping sensation I had of being haunted. At every rustle I whipped round half expecting to find her standing there, backed by the hostile gang. The nervous minutes ticked slowly by, and then at last I spotted Jo. She was tearing across the field. I couldn't understand why she was running so hard. As far as I could tell there was no-one chasing her. She kicked her way through the undergrowth, stopping only to lean down and tear her foot free of some brambles. She was acting as if the hounds of hell were at her heels.

"Janey's . . . on . . . her . . . way," she panted, clutching the breath between each word. "She'll be here . . . any minute now!"

I stared confusedly across the fields. If Janey was coming, she'd have to come on foot but there was no sign of her. Then as if by way of a defiant retort, we heard the high pitched grumble of an unhealthy engine. The only thing between it and us was one sharp hairpin bend. Jo and I instinctively dived into the ditch by the side of the lane. We barely had time to get fully concealed in it when the van screeched to a halt only yards from where we lay hidden. The smell of hot fumes was overpowering. I heard the van doors being slammed and then, to my surprise another car approached and stopped nearby. I hoped it might be the police but it was Mo Mogaran and she was angry.

"Janey, you know that van is dangerous. It's leaking petrol!" she cried, as she came and stood alarmingly close to me and Jo. "I couldn't believe my eyes when

I saw you driving it. I had to ask Bob, here, to chase after you in his car. We've been flashing you to stop for the last mile. Don't you use your mirror?"

"It's leaking oil," retorted Janey. "And I'd thank you to mind your own business. I don't have to ask your permission before I drive my own van, or do I?"

"If you want to blow yourself up, go ahead but I'm more concerned about that cargo of kids you're carrying. The van's a death trap, Janey, and you know it."

Mo's angry words were instantly followed by a chorus of complaints from the gang, who must have been in attendance and who now realized they'd been literally perched on a time bomb. Someone – it sounded like Chelle – even burst into tears with the shock. In the deep murky ditch, Jo and I grinned at one another. I lifted my head and peeped cautiously through the grass to where they were all hotly accusing Janey of putting their lives in mortal danger.

"It's oil," Janey roared at them. "Stop bleating about a drop of oil!"

"It is not oil," said a rather monotonous male voice. I knew it was Mo's car mechanic neighbour, Bob. He often did the repairs on the van. "I looked at that van last week and I told you then it was too dangerous to drive. Mo's right, it's a deathtrap!"

Chelle howled all the louder at hearing this, whilst the others yapped at Janey like angry dogs. She was unmoved. If the gang fancied that they'd brushed shoulders with death, it was of no consequence to Janey Squires. She had more important things to deal with, like finding me and Jo.

"Forget the van," she shouted irascibly. "We've come here to find those runaway kids. I'm going to teach them both a lesson they won't forget in a hurry. Lucy won't get away with making a fool out of me!"

We were too close for comfort, only mere feet away from Janey's wrath. I trembled involuntarily. Mo was trying vainly to calm her down but she wouldn't be easily diverted.

"I know they're here," she cried emphatically. "It may be that I have to kiss goodbye to The Challenge Cup and the prize money, but I'll find that little traitor before I'm finished tonight!"

"You're not causing any more trouble here," replied Mo steadily. "I'm taking you home. If I have to tie you up and put you in the boot, I will. You're not thinking straight, and I'm not leaving you in this mood!"

There was silence while Janey digested this threat. Mo ordered the gang into the car and they obediently went.

"Well, Janey, what's it to be?" she asked with chilling seriousness.

Janey paused. She knew Mo well enough to realize the threat wasn't an empty one. "All right, all right," she muttered. "I'm coming."

Mo laughed triumphantly and went on to the car satisfied that Janey was following. I cautiously watched as Janey hesitated. She fished in her pockets, took out a cigarette and lit it, just as everyone screamed "Don't do that!"

"It's oil," she muttered to herself as she defiantly puffed on the cigarette. She cast a long, expressive stare towards Angelica's empty house. The car sounded as if it was being turned round, the horn was being pipped impatiently. She sighed audibly and, as she turned towards the ditch, I began to lower my head. I half glimpsed her making a sharp movement with her arm, but the whole action was lost to me. I ducked my head into the ditch and didn't move until their car had pulled away. Then we climbed out of the ditch. Janey's fume stenched van was parked so far onto the grassy verge that it was almost against the back of Angelica's stable block. I didn't think Angelica would be very pleased. Wasting no time, Jo and I jogged off down the lane, grateful for Mo's timely intervention, and only too keen to get off the premises.

But all the way to the bus stop something troubled me. I couldn't put my finger on what it was. Jo said it was probably my narrow escape from Janey, but it wasn't that. I just had an inexplicable feeling that something was very wrong at Manor's Hall, something I'd half seen but couldn't quite recall. It puzzled me and nagged at me. I went over the same ground repeatedly. Dance was safely stabled. Mo would see that Janey wouldn't return that night. It was like a jigsaw with the one telling piece missing. I gave it up as lost as we sat on the kerb and waited for our bus. When it arrived, we dragged ourselves exhaustedly upstairs and took over the back seat as we always did. Outside the stubble fields were cast with heavy shadows. I looked at my watch and was surprised to find it was already nine thirty. My parents would be worried, and I hoped they wouldn't ring Janey.

The bus wound its annoyingly slow way through the darkening country lanes with Jo and I sitting in weary silence. Suddenly she leapt to her feet, almost giving me a heart attack in the process.

"What is it?" I gasped. I had this premonition that

she'd discovered what it was that I had been worrying about. Of course it wasn't that at all.

"It's my bracelet. I've dropped it!"

"Oh, is that all?" I sighed disappointedly.

"Is that all?" repeated Jo savagely. "Aunt Cleo only gave it to me this morning. I promised her I wouldn't wear it. I promised her I would take it straight home. It's been in the family for ever and a day. It's valuable!"

"So why didn't you just take it home?" I asked, too tired to be sympathetic.

"Because I was already late in meeting *you* this morning, so I just shoved it on my wrist . . ." Jo's voice trailed dispiritedly away.

The other passengers on the top deck were twisting their heads to see what the fuss was about.

"Jo," I murmured uncomfortably. "Cool off, you'll get us chucked off the bus!"

"I don't care. I'm getting off the bus! I'm going back to find it!"

"You're what?" I almost stuttered. "It's too dark!"

"Luce, I know exactly where to look for it. I bet you it fell off near to where I met you at Manor's Hall. Remember how I got my foot twisted in those brambles and I leant down to free myself? Well, I felt it catch, I just didn't stop to think."

I breathed deeply before somehow managing to resign myself to the miserable trail back to Manor's Hall. "O.K." I muttered. "Let's go back."

We were at least lucky enough to catch another bus almost immediately and it took us speedily to where we'd just come from. That left a walk of about a mile. It was dark, windy and cool. I kept imagining the trouble I would be in when I eventually reached home.

We passed the only detached house on that lonely road, and it looked deserted. I wondered if the occupants would be enjoying themselves at the same "do" Ros and Angelica were at.

At last we reached the private road to Manor's Hall. The starless night was quite black now. Jo was going on about how she wished we had a torch. We tramped into the tight bend with the trees rearing up on each side of us. Then we both stopped and stared. The trees glowed with a flickering orange light they ought not to have possessed. I was confused. There was a low and ominous crackling noise coming from the hollow in which the stables were set. Then, at once, drifting on the wind came the telling, acrid smell of smoke. I knew there and then what I'd been trying to recall, what I'd even half-glimpsed. Janey Squares had thrown away her lighted cigarette.

Chapter Thirteen
To the Rescue

I'd never run faster in all my life than I did towards Manor's Hall that night. The worst part of the fire was roughly contained in the corner of the "L" shaped stable block. It blazed up the walls and leapt from the badly damaged roof in savage tongues of flame. There were four horses inside. I knew because Dance was one of them.

"First of all, Luce, we should get help!" yelled Jo as I tore open the stable doors. I didn't even reply. I dived into the smoky building with one purpose, to save Dance. Jo caught up with me within seconds. I tried to shake her loose as she urgently repeated that we ought to ring for the fire brigade.

"There's no time," I argued desperately. "If we wait, these horses will die."

Jo's hesitation was brief, then she let go of my arm and we made our way into the crackling, smoking building. The first two ponies were stabled very near to the door and we got them out without much bother. I doubted that Dance and Jet would prove as easy to save. Dance was at the furthest point away from us. As we went deeper into the smoke and heat, my eyes watered uncomfortably, but worst of all were the choking coughs we were both developing. Jo motioned towards the buckets along the side of the wall. She slung off her jacket and doused it deeply into the water. I did the same.

"I'll get Jet out," Jo shouted, before we fastened the wet jackets around our faces.

At the far end of the corridor the fire was roaring and spitting like an animal trapped in its lair. Dance was reeling round his box as if trying vainly to dodge the attacking heat. His coat ran with sweat, every muscle and vein looked fit to burst. I slid the bolt, letting the door fall open. He seemed blind to my efforts. In desperation I grabbed his bridle off the rack and darted unwittingly into his box. He was startled and lashed out with a kick that whipped towards me, grazing my hip. I hadn't caught anything like the full force but I was still knocked into the straw. The jacket around my face was jerked loose but it gave me the idea to try and cover his eyes.

Again and again I approached him but each time he shied away. When I got the jacket almost over his head he'd rear, sending it spinning to the ground. I picked it up with a growing sense of hopelessness. The fire was creeping nearer to us. Its scorching unremitting heat was going to force me back. Suddenly, Jo was beside me, her face streaked with grime. She was yelling that there wasn't much time left and she'd managed to get Jet out. Dance's legs had begun to twitch. His panic was turning visibly into exhaustion. I stumbled blindly towards him and thrust the jacket over his eyes. Jo slipped the reins round his neck. We pulled at him but he stood still and trembling, as if on the brink of collapse. I stared despairingly at Jo. I knew there was no time left but just as I was about to admit defeat, the electric cable along the wall caught fire and buzzed like a fuse. The light bulbs above us

103

began to explode like guns being fired. The noise jerked Dance into life. He dragged us out of the burning stable. We half stumbled and half ran with him down the corridor until at last I felt the cool and blustery night air against my scorched skin.

I dropped exhaustedly onto the ground. I was gasping and gulping for oxygen like a fish out of water. I thought I was bound to die as my heart thudded and my brain reeled. I think minutes must have passed before Jo managed to crawl over to where I lay pressed against the cold concrete. The stable roof was collapsing with a cacophony of thuds and crashes. Jo pulled me to my feet and without speaking we stumbled through the garden and up the long steps to Angelica's silent, brooding house. I smashed a window with a heavy stone, but it left jagged edges. Jo began to knock them out only the stone she was using slipped and one of the glass edges split her palm open like paper. She let out a yell as the blood began to pour. It added more nervous urgency to our efforts. I climbed frantically into the room and helped Jo in after me. We knocked into furniture until we found the light switch. Jo was understandably alarmed by the trail of her blood that had marked Angelica's beige carpet but really that damage was the least of our problems. I wrenched up the receiver and dialled 999. My voice was husky from the effects of smoke. I stumbled over my words as I desperately tried to spell out the address to the calm voice on the other end of the line. At last it was done and I replaced the receiver.

The dramatic sirens of the police, ambulance and fire brigade took mere minutes to arrive. They signalled the end to our part in the Manor's Hall fire. In what seemed a bad dream, we were whisked to hospital where Jo was spirited away to have her hand stitched and to be given a tetanus injection. My hip was badly bruised from Dance's kick and apparently we were both suffering from the effects of smoke. I was glad to hear that, despite all they were going to let us go home that night. We waited in a doctor's consulting room for our families to arrive. The first people to burst into the room though, were Angelica and Ros. Angelica looked pale and tired. She appeared to go even paler when she saw the state of me and Jo. We did look like war casualties.

"Are the horses alright? Is Dance . . . ?" I began.

"They're fine, thanks to you two girls. The fire brigade got there before any damage was done to the other buildings. The four horses you rescued are being examined by the vet, but I'm sure they'll recover. I don't know how to thank you."

"Nor do I," said Ros, slipping her arm round my shoulder. "After all, my horse, Jet, was amongst those you saved."

"That was all thanks to Jo," I said.

Jo was half asleep. She yawned wearily and muttered, "I'm sorry about dripping blood over your carpet."

Angelica and Ros were assuring Jo that their carpet was of no consequence when my parents arrived. I almost collapsed with shock because they were hand in hand. Lately they'd gone everywhere as if they had a wall between them. They were rapidly followed by Jo's parents and her Aunt Cleo whose bracelet had been the only reason for our timely return visit. Jo's stunningly handsome brother, Matt, had come along too. Jo ignored them all, curled up on the examination bed and went to sleep. I could never have been so blasé in Matt's company, but then he wasn't *my* brother. The little room was crowded and it rang with voices of concern, alarm and then, as our story unfolded, predictable anger.

"Wait until I get my hands on Janey Squires," exploded my mother. "How could she be so insane as to buy a child a steeplechaser?"

"Actually, he's an excellent horse," said Ros and I smiled gratefully at her.

"I don't know if Janey's choice of him was the result of her expertise or just plain good luck," smiled Angelica. "We'll never know that for certain, but it can't be denied that in choosing Dance she picked a very rare bargain indeed."

"But is he suitable for a child?" asked my father.

"Oh, he's the perfect gentleman when it comes to looking after Lucy," replied Ros. "I would never have been a part of helping them both if I hadn't thought Lucy could manage him."

"Yet it seems Janey Squires chose him with the sole purpose of winning her The Challenge Cup," stated my mother shakily. "She's used us all!"

"Well, fortunately, we've found out about that in time to stop it happening. Lucy can't possibly ride such a big horse in The Challenge Cup. We're all agreed on that."

Everyone nodded their agreement, and once again their unerring confidence that I couldn't possibly ride in such an event, annoyed and hurt me. The Challenge Cup had been the focus for all my energies. It was the indirect reason why Jo and I had nearly been killed that very night and why the gang and Janey would most likely never speak to us again. It seemed ironic that the only person, apart from Jo who believed I could win the cup, was Janey, and most people thought she was mad! I believed they were all underestimating me, just as they always had.

"I suppose that's your final decision," I said tragically.

Angelica said gently, "Oh, Lucy, there'll be other years when you can enter The Challenge Cup. Don't be impatient, your day will come." Then she turned to my parents and with that same placatory sweetness told them I could keep Dance at Manor's Hall. She also informed Jo's parents that there would always be a pony available for Jo to ride. "It's the very least I can do," she smiled.

By the time Angelica swept out of that room, my parents had been talked out of selling Dance, Jo's parents had happily agreed to free riding lessons for Jo, and Aunt Cleo had written off the still missing antique bracelet as "not very important". Angelica was like that. She could storm into these messy situations and, with a mercurial quality, organize us lesser mortals. Only I was disappointed, but I kept that very much to myself.

The following few days were a hectic blur of visitors and numerous renditions of our rescue. We were in the local paper – hailed as heroines, and eventually we were interviewed by the police. They asked if either of us smoked cigarettes which got Jo really paranoid. Afterwards she asked me why I hadn't mentioned seeing Janey throw her cigarette away.

"Well, I can't be a hundred per cent certain," I argued. "Maybe she didn't throw it away. I couldn't tell exactly what she did!"

"What if the police think *we* set fire to the place?"

"They won't!" I said. "They know we risked our

lives to save the horses. Anyway, everyone knows we don't smoke."

Two nights later, Jo came cycling to my house. She burst in on me excitedly. "I've heard that Janey's been taken to the police station for questioning," she blurted out, and it proved to be true enough.

The whole of the town seemed to buzz with rumour, gossip and frivolous speculation about Janey and the Manor's Hall fire. I thought Angelica Kent might be rather pleased by Janey's potential downfall but she said it was nonsense. Janey would never put a horse's life in danger. I agreed with her. Janey had many faults but she truly loved all animals.

With only two nights to go before The Challenge Cup, Kay Davenport unexpectedly rang me. She made it quite clear that the only reason for the call was to relay a message from Janey. I was surprised. I had thought that by now Janey would be languishing in jail. Kay retorted that the police had only wanted to talk to Janey about the van being parked at Manor's Hall. There was no question of her being charged with arson. In fact the fire had been written off by the police as accidental. I was relieved by that news at least. Kay then reminded me that I was dropped from the Long Meadows team. Janey had apparently sent a letter to the organizers informing them of this alteration. Kay rounded off our enjoyable little conversation by saying *she* was going to win The Challenge Cup and thereby put Long Meadows back on the map again! I said, "Good luck to you", in a dry tone, and she said it wouldn't be a case of luck, more sheer spirit and skill.

I had hoped that the fire would have marked the

end of Janey and Angelica's rivalry. Kay's conversation with me implied that it had made it worse.

The next day an article appeared in the local paper. It recounted a very one-sided version of Janey's story. It was told in such an emotive way that it could have made even the most hardened reader stretch for the tissues. The tale of her painful struggle to survive against such cruel odds as millionaire rivals and failing health were set beside a picture of Janey looking melancholy in her empty stable yard. Of course, Janey was feasting on a chance of getting free publicity whilst Angelica ignored any opportunity to answer back, with admirable self control. It was winning Janey some support. People who didn't know her were moved by the story of her desperate fight. The article naturally centred on how Janey was pinning her last hopes on winning The Challenge Cup, and as a result the whole town was gripped by the forthcoming race and all the years of tension it embraced.

I was well enough to ride, and Dance was by now fit enough to be ridden again. I felt sorely left out of all the preparations for the big race. Janine Rich was driving me and Jo mad by swanking around the place, supremely confident of winning. I imagined Kay Davenport would be doing much the same thing at Long Meadows. My situation was made more frustrating by the news that Elspeth Montgomery, who was meant to be riding for Manor's Hall, had broken her arm. I rushed to plead with Angelica and Ros about me taking her place. Without any hesitation they said definitely not! Ros added more gently that in a year or two I would be able to enter as many cross countries as I liked, but at the moment, in her opinion, I was too young and inexperienced.

"Just be patient, Luce," she advised.

Patience was not one of my stronger characteristics. "It's not fair, Jo," I moaned that night, as we lay sprawled around listening to records. "I'm as good a rider as any one of them, aren't I?"

"Yeah," said Jo without any interest.

"It's not fair," I repeated, and I kept on repeating it until Jo said, "Shut up, Luce!"

"Well, it's not. This is what the whole summer has been about. It's the reason why we're not friends with the gang any more, why Pawn isn't still in love with you . . ."

"He is," grunted Jo. "He rang me last night."

"Oh," I said.

Jo sat up. "There's two numbers going free, why don't you use one of them or even both of them and sneak into the race. It's always chaotic on the day."

I laughed at her suggestion, but after a moment or two it began to strike me that it wasn't such a bad idea. "The Challenge Cup" was best described as an organizer's nightmare, what with complaining parents, loud mouthed kids and officious riding school owners.

"I bet I could dodge the stewards and get in easily," I mused. "I could wear the Long Meadows number on one arm and Elspeth's Manor's Hall number on the other. So if anyone saw me, I'd have a fairly good chance of them believing I belonged to one riding school or the other."

"You'd have to keep out of Angelica and Ros's sight," said Jo equally as excited by now. "You could doll up to look older and we could plait Dance's mane and put leg bandages on him. I bet in the muddle no-one would even recognize you!"

110

"We'll do it, Jo," I said.

"There'd be trouble if you won," warned Jo. "You don't belong to either riding school in terms of the race. You're scratched from Long Meadows and you were never entered for Manor's Hall. I doubt they'd give you the cup."

"I won't win. Jet's much faster than Dance. Anyway I'm not bothered about winning," I lied. "I just want to enter . . ."

"For the fun of it," concluded Jo, with a nod of agreement.

I smiled at her. That was it! I was going to ride in The Challenge Cup just for the fun of it. As far as Jo and I could tell there was no possible harm in that.

Chapter Fourteen
Just for the Fun of It

The morning of The Challenge Cup race dawned with a clear sky and the promise of a mellow September day ahead. I pulled on some jeans and a sweatshirt before hiding my best riding clothes in a bag under my bed.

"I'm so thankful that you're not riding today," commented my mother, as we had breakfast. "Every time I think of you in a point to point race on an ex-steeplechaser, I go quite dizzy."

"Why? It is meant for kids."

"Older kids," replied my mother. "It's received a great deal of criticism this year. I don't think that local businessman ought to have donated so much towards the prize money. It's turned a harmless fun-race into a no-holds-barred steeplechase. Someone will get hurt, mark my words."

I gulped my tea. My mother's words were not the ones I would have chosen to hear that particular morning. It made me briefly wonder if I was doing the right thing in sneaking into this race. What if it was harder than I'd imagined? Fortunately, Jo arrived and diverted my attention. We hurried off to Manor's Hall with my parents saying that they'd keep a look-out for us both. I hoped they wouldn't look too hard.

At Manor's Hall, Jet and Janine were both acting

as if the Cup was already won. Jet was prancing around on the end of his lead reign, bursting with hot pride and temperament, while Janine gloated. It annoyed Jo so much that she turned to me and said, "Are you positive Jet's faster than Dance?"

I could only confirm that he was.

"Pity," grunted Jo.

"I thought you didn't want me to win. It'd land us in trouble."

"Well, maybe not win, just beat Janine Rich," replied Jo.

"She'll be in the lead, Jo. I'd bet my life on it!"

Dance did not look the part of a winning horse. He was filthy dirty from rolling in the paddock and he was in a very playful mood. So much so that he gave me and Jo the runaround for twenty minutes before condescending to be caught. I wasn't amused, and I told him as much as I led him into his stable. It was going to be a long hard job to get him clean but Jo and I set to it with grim determination.

It wasn't long before Angelica looked in at us and asked the inevitable question of what were we doing? I told her I wanted to ride Dance to the showground to see how he'd react to the other horses and the crowds. She smiled and was just about to say something when someone called for her and she had to rush off! It was fortunately a hectic morning at Manor's Hall. By the time we'd got Dance clean, the Manor's Hall crowd were ready to set off for the showground. Ros came to find us. I had to tell her the same story I'd just told Angelica. She leaned on the stable door and watched us with an amused and partly sceptical expression before saying, "He's been going to race meetings all his life, Luce. I don't think he needs any more experience at them."

"I know he has," I said uncomfortably. "But not with *me* on him. I want to find out for myself."

Ros shrugged. "Right, well, I'll see you there, then," she said as she left us.

"Phew," groaned Jo. "We'll have to watch out for her. I don't think she swallowed that rubbish you gave her!"

By the time we'd finished grooming Dance, he looked immaculate. His coat shone, his mane was plaited and for the purpose of disguise we'd even dug out some fancy leg bandages to put on him. I changed into my riding gear and then wore my baggy jeans and sweater over the top. By the time we set off for the showground I was nervously excited while Jo was just elated and amused by the smooth way our hilariously clever plan seemed to be succeeding.

I'll admit I had some doubts now that the actual race was drawing so close. I admired Ros and respected her opinions enough to ask myself, was she likely to be wrong about my ability. I thought not, but even if I didn't win I'd show her, Angelica, my parents, the gang and Janey Squires that Dance and I were a force to be reckoned with. Jo was backing me up in my recklessness.

"Stop worrying," she advised me. "It ain't the Grand National, just some potty Pony Club event!"

The show grounds were brimming with lively activity. There were kids, dogs, adults. There were lanes of horse-boxes, tents, ice cream vans, hot dog stands and above all, these were the most snobby looking horses you've ever seen. They were waltzing round with a "don't I look stunning today?"

expression on their equine faces. Dance was no better, except we had to keep a very low profile which didn't suit him. He was very much your high profile type. In fact we spent our time ducking and diving out of the way of my parents, Angelica and Ros. We both agreed that the less they saw of us the better our chances of getting into the collecting ring undetected.

I went to the stewards' tent and asked for my Long Meadows number. It was handed to me without so much as a hesitation, which surprised me considering I'd been dropped from the team! Jo went and got the Manor's Hall number which ought to have gone to Elspeth Montgomery, had she been riding. Jo had to tell them she was Elspeth Montgomery and hope that Angelica hadn't got round to informing them of the change. She hadn't. The number was handed over. Now that we were in firm possession of the two numbers, 105 and 115, I fastened one to each arm, and then Jo and I fell about laughing. We really did think it was a hilarious joke and we congratulated each other on the clever way we were fooling everyone.

There was a list of events during that day but the chief one was of course The Challenge Cup race. As the starting time of three o'clock drew nearer, we came out of hiding to give Dance a pre-race gallop. It was a quick, short and rather sneaky attempt at exercising him, but it did give Dance a chance to stretch his legs. I found him hard to handle but I didn't mention this to Jo as we made our way towards the busy collecting ring. There was an oldish steward at the gate and he was ticking off the number of each rider as they went in. We spotted Janey Squires, dressed in a blaze of colour and looking more like a latter day hippy than a riding school teacher. She had the gang bunched around her like a pack of hounds. Kay was in pride of position on Max, who I didn't think stood a chance.

We hung back rather anxiously waiting for the right moment to enter the collecting ring. It came unexpectedly when a girl on a nervy horse fell off and her horse galloped away. The resulting commotion was our ideal opportunity. I rode single mindedly past the steward.

"Who are you? What's your number?" he yelled.

"105," I called back and I heard Jo yell "115". The steward was shouting and muttering, but I just rode into the throng of riders and kept my head down. I was in!

The mood in the collecting ring was feverish with contained energy. Dance was testy with impatience. This was what he had been bred to do and he grew hot and restless as we waited for the off. I swung him in circles when he pulled too hard against the bit. As the seconds ticked by I grew nervous and even doubtful of my ability to control him. I watched the other competitors with an uneasy sense of being in the wrong place at the wrong time. They were so much older and definitely more professional. A hundred thoughts began to chase across my mind, not least that this was madness. What was I trying to prove? Uncautiously I glanced into the crowd and my gaze flicked anxiously through the many faces until it was met by Ros's concentrated stare. She gaped and frowned at me as if trying to satisfy herself that she wasn't hallucinating. Then she began pushing her way through the spectators. I caught Jo's eye and desperately pointed out what was happening. Jo shot off like a terrier on the attack with the obvious intention of intercepting Ros's progress.

Fortunately we were called to the starting line. I squeezed my knees firmly against the saddle and clutched some of Dance's plaited mane along with the reins. Everyone was crowding each other, and there was a sudden delay when one girl's horse kicked out. I had to turn Dance and again I forgot all caution and looked into the crowd by the rails. This time it was my mother's face that stared back at me. It was frozen solid with horror until she began to slowly and emphatically mouth the words, "Lucy, get out of there! Now!"

I decided a plea of ignorance was my best bet so I mouthed back with a shake of my head, "I can't understand what you're saying."

I threw in a little wave to soften the blow. She must have blabbed the news to my father because he started forward as if he'd had an electric shock. I shot a desperate glance from one side of the course to the other, knowing that if the race didn't start within minutes I would be forced out of it. My dad was battling his way rather violently onto the course when a very burly steward caught hold of him. They rocked backwards and forwards, with my father turning very red and yelling something which I think must have been insulting because the last I saw of him he was being manhandled out of the crowd.

We were called back to the starting line. At last the starter's flag went up. A hush fell. It sliced the air and we were off. We exploded in a tight bunch onto the opening lengths of the course. Dance dragged at the bit and in my initial panic at this furious pace, I pulled against him. We were thundering towards the first jump. I realized with nightmarish terror that we were so crowded by the others that I couldn't even judge our distance to it. Dance nearly left me behind when he took off. We landed heavily. I lurched and bumped in the saddle. The reins were dragged through my fingers and with no aid from me Dance made his move towards the inside rail.

That first jump had dramatically split the bunch. There were six horses ahead of me, all of them were running wide. We were hugging the inside rail and closing the distance, not that I cared. I was clinging to Dance's mane and only thankful that I could at least *see* the second jump. In fact it was looming towards us with stark clarity. We soared into the air, landed smoothly and made ground on the leaders. There was only Kay, Janine and a boy I didn't recognize ahead of us as we galloped down a long hill.

We were charging at break-neck speed towards the blackest looking ditch and bank I've ever seen. I hadn't any idea how we were going to get over it, I know I had a desperate wish that we could approach it more slowly but Dance was by now in sole charge. I was learning just what Ros had meant when she'd called me "inexperienced"! Dance steadied himself as Kay's horse stopped dead. She was caterpulted off, and I shut my eyes fully expecting to join her. Dance leapt onto the bank and off again as if he were carrying a baby on his back. When I opened my eyes it was to find that there was only Janine Rich and Jet ahead of us. Dance seemed content to stay behind Jet until we were about half-way round the last circuit. Then it started to bug him that Jet still had the lead and his stride began to grow even more furious. Jet and Janine seemed unsettled by our inching up to them. They misjudged the penultimate fence. We didn't. We landed abreast. Suddenly, I wanted to win and saw that I could. Side by side with Jet we raced towards the last fly fence. Jet took off first. Dance ignored my wanting to take off with them. He jumped a moment later, almost unseating me, but his timing was exactly right. We landed ahead. I crouched low over Dance's neck as Jet dropped back. Each stride we took left them further behind. We galloped unfettered by competition towards the finishing line and crossed it to an eruption of applause. We'd won.

Even as our pace dropped, people sprang up to us from every side. They shouted "well ridden". "What a marvellous horse!" But their comments flowed over me. I was too busy thanking Dance, kicking my stiff legs free of the stirrups and realizing how much I owed to this horse of mine. He'd seen me through the most daunting ride I'd ever experienced. People were telling me I'd ridden beautifully, but it wasn't true. Dance was the only hero. I looked keenly round for Jo and found her being marched towards me as if she was under arrest. She was caught between Angelica, Ros, my parents, her parents, Janey Squires and Mo Mogaran. They all had identically unsmiling expressions on their faces. Meanwhile one of the judges was asking whom I'd ridden for and I was just about to say 'no-one' when Angelica's voice rose like the sword of Damaclese. "Lucy, how dare you?" she shouted. "How dare you sneak into this event, of all events. You could have been killed."

Then she caught sight of the Manor's Hall number on my left arm and this seemed to excite her even further. "And under the auspices of my riding school," she roared.

Dance inched slowly round as if bored by the fuss. "I beg your pardon, Madam," screeched Janey

119

Squires. "But Lucy rode for Long Meadows. There's *our* number!"

She was right, of course, the Long Meadows number was rather askew but still there for all to gaze at.

"I don't understand," said the judge, with a frown. "Who did you ride for?"

"No-one," I said uncomfortably. "I just wanted to ride . . ." The faces staring back at me could be best described as expressing emotion on a scale from puzzled to mad as hell as I added hopelessly, "just for the fun of it."

The judge ignored me rather rudely and asked a steward to fetch the entry list. My parents pointed out that I had been formally dropped from the Long Meadows team. Angelica Kent pointed out that I had never been entered for the Manor's Hall team, and in the background I caught sight of Janine Rich moving nearer. I kept muttering that I didn't want the cup and didn't care about who got the money, but no-one was listening to me. The steward came quickly back and after the judge had searched down the list and turned a few pages back and forth, he said to Janey, "We haven't received any notice telling us that this girl wasn't representing Long Meadows."

"But I gave it to Pawn to p . . . p . . . post," Janey stuttered.

I was sitting up now. Pawn had a memory like a sieve. It was a well known fact that if you told him to do something he inevitably forgot.

"So was she or was she not riding for Long Meadows?" barked the judge irritably.

Janey paused. The atmosphere clenched. "She most

120

certainly was," replied Janey proudly. "You've had no word to tell you otherwise."

Her eyes searched through the stunned crowd for anyone who dared to contest her claim. There was not one who did. Jo was standing with one hand over her mouth in horrified shock at what we'd done. Angelica's expression was sardonic and cool, while Janey Squires suddenly threw back her head and laughed for all the world to hear.

Chapter Fifteen
Misunderstood?

Tempers cooled eventually. Angelica hadn't really minded about losing the cup or the money. Her main concern was that I could have been hurt. Ros was similarly as proud as can be of Dance but she told me in as many variations known to mankind that I was a complete idiot! Neither was I looking forward to the Awards Ceremony at the town hall where the Cup and the money were due to be handed over to Janey Squires.

"I didn't mean her to get the money," I groaned, but I was wasting my time. No-one had any sympathy. Jo and I had come to terms with the knowledge that we'd given our enemy, Janey, the prestigious first prize. I blamed Jo, she blamed me, but most people blamed us both equally.

No-one could dispute Janey's claim to the Challenge Cup. Her letter to the judges informing them that I was dropped from the team could no doubt have been discovered in Pawn's shirt pocket, but it was of no earthly use there. I'd made Janey's wish come true, but the circumstances could never have been more ironic.

As a result, the night of the Awards Ceremony was tainted by reluctance and resentments. I considered getting unexpectedly ill so as not to have to attend but

Jo was of the opinion that I ought to see it through. I thought this was rich coming from her. After all it was I who would have to go on to that stage with Janey and receive our prize.

The only good news was that my parents had been much closer since the Manor's Hall fire. When they took me and Jo to the Awards Ceremony they at least were in high spirits. I was dreading the whole thing and felt even worse once we were inside. It was crowded, and the Long Meadows team were all there, in pride of position.

"Can't she go on to the stage by herself?" I asked huffily.

Not if she keeps drinking that punch she can't," joked my father, and we all glanced across the room to where Mo and Janey were standing rather unsteadily beside the bowl of alcoholic punch.

"You did ride for Long Meadows," smiled Angelica.

"But I didn't mean to, it was by accident . . ."

"You've only yourself to blame," interrupted my mother, and Jo dragged me away before the lecture had its umpteenth re-run. We fled bang into Kay and Dee. Kay seemed none the worse for her dramatic head first dive into the ditch. In fact she was her usual charming self. Dee was free and easy with her insults, as she so often was when Kay was beside her. "Traitors," she hissed. "What's it like to belong to the other side?"

"Buzz off," smiled Jo calmly.

"I think you've made a big mistake in leaving Long Meadows," commented Kay smugly. "Janey has big plans. It's the start of a whole new era for us. We're buying new ponies and building more stables."

"I'll believe it when I see it," I said.

"What's she going to pay for it with – monopoly money?" retorted Jo playfully.

Kay was annoyed and shoved Jo who instantly retaliated by shoving her back.

I got between them. "Don't," I said. "Not here!"

Kay paused and seemed to agree on the inappropriateness of the situation. "Oh, you'll both keep," she said with deep feelings, and they stalked off.

"Did we once used to be friends with them or was I dreaming it?" asked Jo with a sigh.

"I don't know why they're mad at us. After all we've helped put their beloved Long Meadows back on the map. Janey's getting £1,500 tonight, and that's all thanks to us!"

"We'll have to watch out for Kay from now on. She's got a long memory . . ."

"Like an elephant," I added with a grin.

People began to take up their places as the microphones were tested. I told Jo I might disappear into the downstairs toilets and sort of accidentally miss out on the ceremony. She agreed to cover for me.

I slipped quietly away, down the dark winding stairs that led into the fortunately empty ladies room. I brushed my hair and told myself I was doing the right thing when I suddenly heard Janey's voice outside. I darted rapidly into the far cubicle and gently pulled the door shut. She was the last person I wanted to confront.

"They're cutting me dead out there, as if I was some kind of monster," she was saying for all the world to hear as she slammed into the room. Nervously, I squeezed myself against the back of the cubicle, between the loo and the wall.

124

It was Mo's voice that replied. "You've never cared before. What's the difference this time?"

"I'm not deceived by them. They think worse of me now than they ever did before. It didn't matter quite so much when I was the loser, but now I've got what I fought for and I can't help asking myself, did I go too far?"

"That's not like you, Janey," laughed Mo.

"Do you think I'm made of stone? I have my regrets too. Everything I did was for the purpose of winning The Challenge Cup. I caused a fire. I put lives in danger. I went too far, Mo. I can see that now. It's scared me."

"It was an accident. No-one thinks otherwise."

"Of course it was," retorted Janey with a bitter laugh. "But there's no denying that I caused it all to happen. It was because I didn't want my precious stables to fold. I didn't want Angelica Kent to prosper where I'd failed."

'Well, the Cup is rightfully yours and you're back in business so you've got what you wanted, haven't you?" asked Mo.

"No, I haven't. There's a room full of hostile people out there who think I'm a crazy woman. They don't understand I was fighting for the only thing I have, Long Meadows. They misunderstand, and tonight it matters, Mo. It matters that Lucy will probably refuse to set foot on that stage with me, and that will wound me deeper than any of their small minded comments ever could."

Mo sighed wearily. "You have to face that, Janey, and maybe I ought to remind Lucy that it was you who picked her that horse."

"I don't blame her," said Janey. "I'm just sorry I

put her through so much and even endangered her and Jo's lives. I was proud of her when she rode Dance over that finishing line, not because of the Cup or the money, but because I'd picked the horse, and in the beginning we'd taught her to ride."

"Lucy knows that," replied Mo. "She might belong to Manor's Hall from now on but she won't forget where she started from."

Janey grunted as if she thought I probably could and would. They muttered something which I didn't quite catch and left the room. I waited for a few hard, pensive minutes and then I made up my mind and ran up the stairs to rejoin Jo. The Challenge Cup was being announced.

"Hey, Luce, hadn't you better disappear?" Jo muttered but I shook my head.

My name was called and so I went forward and climbed the stairs onto the stage. Janey followed more slowly, she looked old and tired now, just as any harmless aging spinster might look. All her imperious, dangerous energy was worn down. There was nothing sharp or severe about her tonight. She was just vulnerable and poignant. The applause was predictably scattered and half-hearted for this woman who most of the town berated. The judge gave her the cheque and I took the small silver cup that had been the focus of so much trouble and so many hopes. To my surprise Janey held her hand out to me and I took it in mind.

We parted company and I went back to Jo who said sarcastically, "That was very touching!"

I didn't reply. I didn't even plan to tell Jo what I'd overheard Mo and Janey saying. I reckoned Jo would call me soft. Perhaps I was. All I knew was that my previously black and white feelings about Janey had been thrown into a big colourful muddle. I'd come at last to feel sorry for her, glimpsing a side to her rarely seen and it had touched me. I tried to shrug it all off as I walked across the darkening car park. It was, after all, over.

My dad caught up with me, and put his arm round my shoulders. "I'm proud of you, Luce," he said, much to my surprise. "You did the right thing tonight by going onto that stage with Janey."

"I thought you were the one who was wanting to kill her," I said.

"That's a slight exaggeration," he smiled. "I certainly don't approve of the woman's methods but I think, given the circumstances, that it's only right we forgive and forget."

I wondered how many others would agree with him, but all that really mattered for the moment was that I did. Jo and I climbed into his car and as it pulled out of the car park we passed the gang and Janey. Jo waved cheekily at them but I kept my eyes firmly ahead.

My mother had heard the story that Janey intended to buy new ponies and was all set to make dramatic changes to Long Meadows. She also told us she'd heard a rumour that following the publicity about Janey's difficulties, the businessman who'd put up The Challenge Cup money, had offered her financial backing. My dad thought this was probably frivolous gossip, but it certainly set my imagination racing. Not that I thought it would affect Angelica. Manor's Hall was as secure as the Rock of Gibraltar. I was convinced of that.

Jo was tutting at me. "This is all because of you,

Luce. I told you not to win The Challenge Cup, didn't
I?"

"You told me to beat Janine Rich," I said with
playful indignation, "which is what I did."

"I think you may have done a bit more than that,"
said my mother quietly.

I ran my hand over the smooth silver cup beside
me, and I remembered some of the cost of winning
it, and the big changes it had brought about. Janey
had her chance of survival now, I had inadvertently
been the one to give her it. I wasn't sorry, in fact it
was why I smiled to myself as the car sped through
the darkness.